rhcbooks.com

ISBN 978-0-7364-4281-7 (hardcover)
ISBN 978-0-7364-4280-0 (paperback)

Printed in the United States of America

10 9 8 7 6 5 4 3 2 1

DISNEY · PIXAR

TURNING RED

The Junior Novelization

Adapted by Cynthea Liu

Random House 🏠 New York

Chapter 1

The number-one rule in Meilin Lee's family? Honor. Your. Parents. They are the supreme beings who gave you life, who sweated and sacrificed to put a roof over your head, food on your plate . . . like, so much food—an *epic* amount of food. The least you could do in return was every single thing they asked. Some people might say, "Be careful. Honoring your parents sounds great, but if you take it too far . . . well . . . you might forget to honor yourself!"

Luckily, Meilin did not have that problem. She did her own thing and made her own moves 24/7, 365. She wore what she wanted, said what she wanted, and did not hesitate to do spontaneous cartwheels if she felt so moved. Now that it was 2002 and she was thirteen, Meilin was officially an adult (at least, according to her Toronto Transit streetcar pass).

One bright and sunny morning, Mei arrived at Pearson Middle School. The day was like any other. Mei wore her glasses and a cardigan, and she rocked sneakers with a favorite pair of pink ankle socks. She ran up the steps, armed with her flute case covered with stickers that said things like THIS GIRL LOVES MATH and SAVE THE WHALES. A digital pet game dangled from her backpack strap. Mei burst through the front doors and spotted one of her besties, Miriam, standing by her locker.

"Miriam!" Mei called.

Miriam rushed over. "Aye!" she said. They did a special handshake, bumped rears, and laughed.

Just then, Priya, another friend of Mei's, showed up beside them. Her face was buried in a teen vampire novel as they all began to walk together. "Yo," she said.

Before Mei could respond, she was interrupted by a girl yelling in Korean at a bunch of hallway litterers. That could only be Abby.

"Abby!" Mei called.

Abby turned. "Wassup, Mei?" She ran to join them.

"Ready to change the world?" Mei said.

The four girls wiggled their fingers together.

"So ready!" Miriam replied.

"I was born to do this," Priya said matter-of-factly.

"Let's burn this place to the ground!" Abby screamed.

The school day began, and Mei, as usual, was on her game.

During math class, she was the first to raise her hand. "Y equals negative four!"

During French, Mei spoke with perfect pronunciation. *"J'aime le fromage blanc!"*

In geography, she called out the correct answer: "Manitoba, Alberta, and Saskatchewan!"

Music was a cinch. Mei rocked her flute while her classmates winced.

Mei did not mess around in grade eight. Her math teacher described her as a "very enterprising, mildly annoying young lady." Kids would probably call her a major weirdo. Tyler, a boy Mei wanted nothing to do with, called her an overachieving dork-narc. But name-calling didn't bother Mei one bit. She accepted and embraced all labels.

Finally, the school bell rang, and Mei pushed her way past other students leaving the school building. "Comin' through!" she said.

Miriam, Priya, and Abby followed close behind as Mei went outside.

"Share the sidewalk, people!" called Mei.

The friends walked together until they reached Daisy Mart, a convenience store.

Miriam gasped. "Mei-Mei-Mei-Mei!" She grabbed Mei's backpack and yanked her backward. "Come see this!"

Miriam dropped to the ground so they couldn't be seen through the store windows. "C'mon!" She crawled past the shop's front door. Mei, Priya, and Abby quickly ducked and did the same. Then, one by one, they peeked through a window.

"Mir—" Mei said, peering in. She had no idea what they were supposed to be looking at.

But Abby and Priya saw. There he was—a gorgeous, scruffy-looking seventeen-year-old clerk, working behind the counter. Abby and Priya sighed together.

Miriam could stare at him for hours. *"Mmm . . . Devon."*

Mei frowned.

Abby watched Devon adjust a sign on the counter. "My mom cuts his hair at the salon, and I've felt it—it's very soft!"

"Whoa," Priya said. "Can I have some?"

"Yeah, Abby," Miriam said. "Hook a sister up!"

"Ew!" Meilin pulled away from the window. "He looks like a hobo!"

"A hot hobo!" Abby said.

Mei reached into her backpack. "May I remind you what real men look like?" She whipped out a copy of *Tween Beat* magazine.

Her friends gasped. "4*Town," they said in unison.

Mei opened the magazine. "Yes! 4*Town!" She pointed at pictures of the boy band members and listed some of their unique qualities and interests. "Jesse went to art school. Tae Young fosters injured doves. Robaire speaks French. And Aaron T. and Aaron Z. are, like, really talented, too!"

She closed the magazine. "We are 4*Townies, remember?" She held up four fingers to the heavens to emphasize her point. "Ride or die!"

Priya sighed. "Yeah, but tickets to 4*Town are, like, a bajillion dollars, and Devon's right here."

"And free!" Abby added.

Mei rolled her eyes. Just then, a streetcar made a stop nearby. "I gotta go," she said.

"Wait!" said Miriam. "We're going karaokeing today—"

"Come with us," Priya said.

Mei turned to stare at her friends. They were all making puppy-dog faces at her. Abby and Miriam whimpered. "Pleeeeeeease?" Priya said.

Mei thought about her mother waiting for her at the family temple. "I can't," she said, though she was torn. "It's cleaning day."

"Mei," Miriam said, "every day is cleaning day. Can't you just get one afternoon off?"

Mei raised an eyebrow. "But I like cleaning. Plus, I got this new feather duster, and omigosh, you guys, it picks up so much dirt. It's bananas!"

"Fine, I'll let you go," Miriam said, "if you can pass the gauntlet." She stood on the sidewalk between Mei and the streetcar, then gestured toward Priya and Abby. "Come on—"

Priya and Abby began beatboxing.

"Mir, not now," Mei protested.

Miriam hip-bumped Mei. "You can't resist it," she teased, then broke out some funky dance moves. She laughed. "Come on! You know you want to."

Priya and Abby's beatboxing intensified.

Mei sighed as she set down her flute case and backpack.

"Here we go. . . ." Miriam began to sing, and before Mei knew it, they were all singing and dancing to one of their favorite 4*Town songs.

Mei belted out the lyrics with as much gusto as she could muster. When they finished, Miriam handed her a 4*Town CD. "And here's your reward," she said.

"O.M.G., Mir." Mei held the CD to her chest. "I'll guard it with my life." She kissed the CD over and over again. "Thankyouthankyouthankyouthankyouthankyou!"

She gave Miriam a hug, and they each held up four fingers.

"4*Town!" Mei said.

"4-evah!" everyone chorused, wiggling their fingers together.

Mei picked up her things and ran for the streetcar. "We'll karaoke another time. I promise!" she called.

"Okay, sure, Mei!" Miriam said.

"It'll be on me!" she yelled back. "The snacks, the tunes . . ."

"Wooo," said Priya.

"You're my jam, girl!" Abby said.

Mei got on board, then waved from a back window as the streetcar pulled away.

Priya watched her go, thinking of how Mei was always so eager to please her mother. "She's so brainwashed," she said to the others.

Chapter 2

When the streetcar pulled to a stop, Mei hurried to get off. She was late, and even though she knew she was her own person, a value she held dearly, she knew she had other people who counted on her—namely, her mom. Mei dashed through the gateway to Toronto's Chinatown, passing shoppers and produce stands along the way.

"'Scuse me!" She ran past a guy holding a pastry box.

"Whoa," the guy said. *"Why are you running so fast?"* he added in Cantonese. *"Don't run!"*

Mei dodged bikes and bins of vegetables as though her life depended on it. Up ahead, two plumbers crossed the sidewalk, carrying a heavy load of pipes. Mei threw the 4*Town CD and the flute case into the air. She somersaulted under the pipes and then caught the CD and flute perfectly as she booked it home.

She ran past a lady holding a plant. "Hello, Meilin!"

"How's it going?" Mei said.

A man carrying a wooden crate passed by. A piece of

fruit fell from the crate, and Mei scooped it up. She tossed it back to the man without missing a beat.

"Thank you, Meilin!" he said.

Mei kept running and reached an intersection. She stopped to look both ways before crossing the street and caught her breath. She was almost there!

At last, she arrived at an old Chinese temple—the Lee Family Temple, *her* temple. Two guardian statues of red pandas flanked the entrance. Mei paused to touch each statue.

"Hey, Bart," Mei said. "Hey, Lisa."

She passed through the grand gate and crossed the small courtyard where Mr. and Mrs. Gao played chess.

"Hello, Meilin!" Mrs. Gao said.

Mei smiled at the couple. "Still down for a rematch, Mr. Gao?"

"Bring it, Lee!" Mr. Gao said. "What a good girl."

Mei entered the gift shop and hung her backpack on a hook. She set her flute case on the counter and affixed a badge to her sweater that read MEILIN LEE, ASSISTANT TEMPLE KEEPER. Then she stopped for a moment to bow to the portraits of her ancestors.

Mei found her mother, Ming, kneeling in front of an altar. Above the altar was a tapestry depicting a beautiful woman dressed in traditional Chinese robes and flanked by two guardian red panda spirits. Ming rose from the floor when she heard Mei approaching. "Mei-Mei! There you are!"

Ming was tall, elegant, and practically ageless. A badge on her lapel matched Mei's: MING LEE, TEMPLE KEEPER.

"Hey, Mom," Mei said.

Ming approached Mei and cradled her face. She studied Mei closely. "You're ten minutes late. What happened? Are you hurt? Are you hungry? How was school today?"

"Killed it, per usual," Mei said.

"That's my little scholar," Ming replied. "Today, honor student. Tomorrow, UN secretary general! The ancestors would be so proud."

Ming and Mei kneeled at the altar. Ming lit incense for each of them.

"Sun Yee," Ming said solemnly, "revered ancestor, guardian of the red pandas—"

Mei opened one eye to peek at the tapestry of her serene ancestor.

"—we humbly thank you," Ming continued, "for protecting and guiding us."

Mei glanced at her mother as she prayed.

Ming's gaze met hers. "Especially Mei-Mei," she said.

They both closed their eyes, and Mei finished the prayer. "May we continue to serve and honor you and this community."

"Always," they said in unison, then bowed.

Ming and Mei went out to the temple's courtyard. Outside, the wind rustled and birds chirped. They took it all in with a cleansing breath. The moment was peaceful. The temple was their special place.

"You ready?" asked Ming.

Mei cracked her knuckles. "Let's do this."

They grabbed the cleaning supplies and tapped their brooms together like hockey players about to hit the ice. Then they cleaned and scrubbed and polished everything in sight, including Bart and Lisa, the red panda statues. They even chased off some teenagers who were trying to graffiti the place.

"You good-for-nothin' hosers," Mei shouted at them.

"I'm telling your mothers," Ming threatened.

At last, a tour group arrived, and Ming escorted the visitors through the temple. She gestured toward the tapestry of Sun Yee. "Our most revered ancestor, Sun Yee, was a scholar, poet, and defender of animals! She dedicated her life to the creatures of the forest, especially—"

Mei popped out in a red panda costume made of cardboard.

"—the red panda!" Ming finished.

"Ta-da!" Mei said.

The tour group oohed and aahed as they snapped photos.

Ming explained that Sun Yee loved the red panda for its fiery coat and mischievous nature. "Ever since," Ming said, "the red panda has blessed our family with good fortune and prosperity."

"And it can bless yours, too!" Mei said.

She passed around a donation box as the tourists applauded.

Ming and Mei ran tour after tour until their shadows grew long as the sun began to set. At last, they escorted the final group out.

"Bye-bye!" Ming said, waving.

"See you next time," said Mei.

They closed the temple gate doors, leaned against them, and sighed with relief. What a day!

"Gimme five," Ming said as they walked toward their house, which was secured by a separate gate on the temple grounds.

Mei smiled at her mother and slapped her a high five, happy to be finished for the night.

At home, Mei's father, Jin, cooked in the kitchen. He chopped, seasoned, and boiled until his glasses fogged up from the steam.

In the living room, Ming and Mei sat on the couch and folded dumplings as they watched their favorite soap opera, *Jade Palace Diaries*.

On the TV, the male lead embraced the leading lady, who was clearly up to no good.

"I want you to stay with me forever," the man said.

Ming groaned. "Hai! He should have listened to his mother and married Ling-Yi."

She folded the last dumpling.

"Totally," Mei said. "Sui-Jyu is so two-faced." She held out a tray for her mother, who set her dumpling on it.

"She's just using him to get to the throne," Ming said. "She'll probably stab him on their wedding night."

"Tsk! You know it, Mom." Mei took the tray of dumplings to her father, who inspected each one. "Hmm," he murmured. "Perfect!"

"Yes!" Mei said.

Pop music emanated from the TV, which caught Mei's attention. A commercial was playing. "You've heard their hits," the narrator said as five dancers came on screen. "You've seen their moves. Now you get to experience them—live! The worldwide pop sensation 4*Town will be kicking off their North American tour! Tickets on sale now!"

Mei's knees suddenly felt weak. She gripped the couch for support. "Omigosh!"

Ming grimaced. "Who are these . . . hip-hoppers?" She turned to look at Mei. "And why are they called Four-Town if there are five of them?"

"I dunno," Mei said. "Some of the kids at school like 'em."

"You mean Miriam?" Ming turned back to the TV. "That girl is . . . odd."

Mei's face fell. Miriam was totally normal. Why couldn't her mom like her friends?

"Dinner's ready!" Jin called.

Ming rose from the couch. As she passed her daughter, she took Mei's chin in her hand and smiled fondly. Mei smiled back.

Then Mei gave the TV one last wistful glance. She hummed part of a 4*Town tune, knowing her mother just wouldn't understand, before she joined her parents at the table.

Chapter 3

In her bedroom, Mei sat at her desk, wearing her head-phones. Her shelves were neatly organized with stuffed animals, trophies, books, and framed photos of her family. Her bed was made, and motivational posters adorned the walls. While Mei did her math homework, she listened to the 4*Town CD that Miriam had given her. Her mind began to wander, and soon she was doodling a face in the margins of her assignment. She paused. The face looked familiar.

"Hmm," Mei said to herself. "Kinda looks like . . . Devon."

She snorted with disgust. "I don't get what Mir sees in him. He's not THAT cute. . . ."

She continued to draw. Maybe his shoulders were kinda nice. His eyes . . . were . . . fine.

Mei stopped. She took off her headphones.

Suddenly, she imagined her doodle of Devon seated on a rock, with a bird perched on his finger. He smiled at her and WINKED.

Mei's eyes widened. What was she thinking? She picked up the notebook but couldn't take her eyes off the picture she had drawn. She swiveled away from her desk. Something was wrong. She was *feeling* something.

She held the notebook to her chest, got out of her chair, and oh-so-nonchalantly moved away from her desk. She sank to the rug and leaned against her bed.

She put the notebook on the floor. Again, she couldn't resist. She picked up the notebook and rolled under her bed like a secret agent.

She drew another image. This time, something new.

When Mei finished, she studied the drawing. It was Devon and Mei, and he was gazing into her eyes as they clasped hands while sitting on a unicorn. Mei flushed.

She turned the page and drew more. Way more. She started to sweat. Her breathing became labored. Before she knew it, she had filled the entire notebook.

"Mei-Mei?"

Mei jumped at the sound of her mom's voice and bumped her head on the underside of the bed. "Ow!" She scrambled out and sat on her bed, trying to look as casual as possible. Just as her mother was opening the door, Mei spotted the corner of her notebook poking out from under the bed. She gasped.

Ming came into Mei's bedroom holding a tray of sliced apples. "Do you want a snack?" she asked.

Mei wore a pained smile, and she was sweating again.

"Cool, great, thanks!" *Don't look at the notebook,* Mei thought. *Don't look at the notebook.*

Ming stared at her daughter. She saw the sweat and knew something wasn't right. Then she saw Mei glance furtively toward the floor. Ming spotted the notebook. She set the tray on the nightstand and picked up the notebook.

"Is this your homework?" Ming said.

Mei let out a nervous laugh.

Ming opened the notebook and quickly realized it was *not* Mei's homework. "Oh . . ."

"Mom, don't!" said Mei.

But it was too late. Ming turned the page.

"Do not—" Mei said. "Mom!"

"Oh my," Ming remarked. "What . . . what is—" She turned another page. "HUH?" Then another. "What?" Her expression morphed into one of absolute horror. "Oh . . . huh? UGH! Mei-Mei!" Now Ming was scared out of her mind. "What is this?"

"It's nothing!" Mei said. "Just a boy. He's no one—"

"A BOY?" Ming held up a drawing of Devon moving in to kiss Mei.

Mei gasped.

"Who is he?" Ming exclaimed. "Did he do these things to you?"

Mei tried to yank the notebook from her mother, but Ming wouldn't let go.

"No," Mei said. "It's just made-up, Mom! It's not real—" The notebook ripped.

Ming squinted at a torn drawing of Devon in her hands. "That hat . . . is that . . . the sketchy clerk from Daisy Mart?"

Before Mei could answer, Ming whirled around and stormed out of the room, blind with rage.

"Mom!" Mei called after. "No!"

Minutes later, the Lee family sedan screeched to a halt in the Daisy Mart parking lot. Ming got out of the car, and Mei jumped out from the passenger side.

"No-no-no-no!" Mei cried as she followed her mother into the store.

The door chimed, announcing their arrival. A bunch of teenagers who were hanging out stared at Ming and Mei as Ming marched toward the counter, her heels clicking. Mei caught a glimpse of someone she knew. *Oh, no!* Tyler, from Mei's school, was there.

"Oh, snap!" Tyler said.

Mei begged her mother to stop, but she was already making a beeline for the counter. Mei followed. "Mom, no!" Everyone in the store gathered to see what was happening.

When Ming got to Devon, she pointed a finger at him. "YOU!"

Devon fell back in his chair with surprise.

"What've you done to my Mei-Mei?" Ming demanded.

Devon seemed confused. "Uh . . . who?"

"Meilin Lee," Tyler crowed. He pointed at her. "Right here!"

All heads turned to Mei.

Mei swallowed.

"I should report you to the police!" Ming seethed as she leaned over the counter. "How old are you?" She eyed Devon up and down. "Thirty?"

"I'm . . . seventeen?" Devon replied, giving her a quizzical look.

Ming turned to Mei. "See? See? This is what happens when you don't wear sunblock and do drugs all day!" She turned to Devon again. "She's just a sweet, innocent child! How dare you take advantage of her!"

Ming reached into her jacket pocket.

Mei gasped. She found her voice again. "Mom, noooooooo!"

Ming pulled out Mei's drawings and slammed them onto the counter. Everyone got closer for a better look.

The top picture was a drawing of Devon as a *merman*.

Tyler snickered.

"Wha-a-at?" Devon said, confused.

Mei was practically hyperventilating from embarrassment.

"What a weirdo!" Tyler said, pointing at Mei.

"What a stalker," a girl whispered to her friend.

Devon stared at the drawing, then looked at Mei.

With nowhere to hide, Mei averted her gaze. Her cheeks burned.

The laughing got louder.

Then her mother made it worse: she whipped out some incense and waved it like she was conducting an exorcism. "Begone . . . hoodlum!"

More laughter.

Ming planted the incense in a counter display, then marched Mei out of the store.

Ming and Mei got into their car. Ming slammed her door shut with satisfaction.

Mei sat in the passenger seat and wilted with shame. *How could my mother do this to me? Wait a second,* she thought. *This wasn't Mom's fault.* Mei realized she was the one who had made it look like she was being *violated* as a minor! Her mother was just doing her job. *You are stupid, stupid, stupid!* she berated herself.

"Thank goodness I was here," Ming said. "That degenerate won't come near you again."

She tucked a strand of hair behind Mei's ear and placed a hand on her shoulder. "Now, is there anything else I should know about, Mei-Mei?"

Mei clenched her hands into fists. "Nope." She faked a smile. "All good."

When Mei returned home, she got ready for bed, then screamed into her pillow.

She sat up and chastised herself with harsh whispers.

"You sicko! What were you THINKING?" She roiled with regret. "Why would you draw those things? Those horrible things!"

She paced the room, trying to think of a way out. "It's fine—you'll move to another city, change your identity . . ."

Then she sat on her bed and cradled her honor roll certificate. "You don't deserve this. You're just a hormonal CAVEMAN." She tore up the paper. "Just like the rest of 'em!"

Mei grabbed a photo of herself and her mother from the nightstand. Feeling like a ball of mixed emotions, she wept. "Mommy . . ." She stroked the frame as though she were petting it. "I'm so sorry!"

She stood in front of her floor mirror and tried to get herself together. "You are her PRIDE and JOY," she said to her reflection, "so act like it!"

Mei slapped her own face. Then she grabbed her notebook, ripped up the pages, and stuffed them into her trash can.

She took a deep breath, looked at the mirror once more, and pointed at herself, dead serious. "This will never . . . happen . . . again."

She turned out the lights, dove into bed, and curled up under the covers.

But her nightmare of a day wasn't over . . . *yet.*

That night, while Mei slept, the courtyard was calm. The chimes swayed. Light spilled from the candles on the altar in the temple, where Sun Yee looked out from her tapestry hanging on the wall. A gust of wind snuffed out the candles, and then there was darkness.

Rain began to patter against the window. As lightning flashed, Mei stirred in her sleep.

She dreamed of the stone statues that guarded the temple. In her dream, they were bathed in an eerie red light. Lightning flashed again. The guardian pandas' eyes glowed white; then the statues exploded, sending two columns of white light heavenward. Hundreds of red pandas poured over the edges of the temple roof, like rats fleeing a sinking ship.

The moon glowed red.

Mei turned in her bed, clutching her pug, Wilfred, her favorite stuffed animal. Her dream took bizarre twists and turns. She dreamed of Devon, shaped like a sushi nigiri, flopping helplessly and pleading for her help. She dreamed of weird man-flowers blooming, revealing the faces of 4*Town's members. More images flooded her dreams: photos of ancestors, a dead bird, a pair of shattered eyeglasses, a horse with a snake tongue, a worm in two pieces squirming on the ground.

Last but not least, above the temple altar, the two red panda spirits from Sun Yee's tapestry opened their eyes. Their eyes glowed red as they leaped out of the tapestry, free at last.

Chapter 4

When Mei woke the next morning, she could hear her mother calling down the hall outside her bedroom. "Mei-Mei!" she said.

Mei rubbed her eyes. Sounds from the radio echoed throughout the house. An announcer said, "We've got a beautiful day out there, folks, after last night's unusually stormy weather. But now it's blue skies for the rest of the week."

In the kitchen, Ming made Mei's bowl of rice porridge. Atop the porridge, she arranged eggs and veggies to make a smiley face. "Are you up?" she called to Mei. She placed a mushroom in the middle of the face, making a perfect nose. "Breakfast is ready!" She took the porridge to the table, where Jin was already seated and eating.

Ming set the bowl down and also put a box of donut holes on the table before sitting.

Jin reached for a donut. "Mmm—"

Ming slapped his hand away. "Ay-yah! No sugar!" The donuts were for Mei-Mei.

Mei got out of bed. "Coming!" She headed for the bathroom, and the scent of breakfast wafted to her nose. "Mmm . . . porridge . . ." She yawned and stepped in front of the sink. In the mirror, she saw a giant furry red form.

The enormous furry thing leaned down to stare at itself. Its big brown eyes went wide.

Mei stared at the mirror. Why did her reflection look like a . . . a . . . *giant . . . red . . . panda*? "Aahhhh!" she screamed.

Alarmed, Ming turned from her breakfast. Jin swiped a donut while she wasn't looking.

In the bathroom, Mei backed her big body into the wall. She gaped at herself in the mirror again. *Fur, teeth, whiskers, claws?*

"This isn't happening," Mei said to herself. "This isn't happening!" She pushed her furry cheeks and clutched her belly fat. She sniffed the air—something did not smell right. She raised an arm and took a whiff of her hairy armpit. *"Bleagh!"*

Tears welled in her eyes. She pawed at her face. "Wake up, wake up, wake up. . . ."

"Mei-Mei?" Ming called.

Mei gasped.

"Is everything okay?"

Her mother was right outside the bathroom door.

Mei grew frantic. "DON'T COME IN HERE!" She spun around, and her bushy tail knocked toiletries off the sink. Her mother couldn't see her like this. *No one* could see her like this.

"Mei-Mei?" Ming said again. She heard the sound of crashing objects. "What's going on, honey? Are you sick?"

Jin gulped down another donut before he got up from the kitchen table and made his way toward Ming in the hall.

"Is it a fever?" Ming continued. "A stomachache? Chills? Constipation—"

"No," Mei said.

"Wait," Ming said. "Is it *that* . . . ?"

Jin stopped in his tracks in the hallway.

"Did . . . the . . . did the red peony *bloom*?"

Jin walked backward until he was out of sight.

"NO!" Mei said. *Wait.* "Maybe?" she said meekly.

Ming sucked in a breath, surprised. "But it's too soon!" She had to do something to help. "Don't worry, Mei-Mei! I'll get everything you need." She accidentally backed into a vase and saved it just in time before running into another room. "Mommy's here!" Then she called to her husband. "Jin! Jin! It's happening!"

In the bathroom, Mei frantically looked around for an escape. She tried squeezing her giant head through the window, knocking over more bottles. "C'mon, please!" She somehow stepped into the toilet and also flushed it. There was no way she could get out through the window. Her head was too big.

"Mei-Mei!" her mother called. "I'm coming! I'm coming!"

"No!" Mei said. She jumped into the tub and pulled the curtain shut just as Ming rushed in, carrying a box full of toiletries. She set the box on the sink counter and started rummaging inside. "It's going to be okay!"

In the bathtub, Mei freaked out. "NO, IT'S NOT!" she seethed. "WILL YOU JUST GET OUT?"

Mei clapped her paws over her whiskery mouth. She couldn't believe she had just yelled at her mother.

"Excuse me?" Ming said.

"I—I didn't mean that!" Mei said quickly as she dissolved into a blubbering mess. "I'M A GROSS RED MONSTER!" she wailed. "WAAAAH!" Mei pulled at her furry cheeks. "Stop it," she said to herself. Her mother couldn't know what had happened to her. "Stop talking!" She slapped herself in the face with a *fwoomph!*

Ming did her best to remain calm. She cleared her throat as she unpacked the box. "Mei-Mei, I know this is upsetting, but we are going to get through this together. She took out many items one by one. "I have ibuprofen . . . vitamin B . . . a hot water bottle . . . and . . . *pads.*" She stacked them on the sink counter in rapid succession. "Regular, overnight, scented, unscented, thin, ultrathin, ultrathin with wings . . ."

"Uh-huh," Mei said. "Awesome. Just leave them by the sink."

"Mei-Mei?" Ming faced the closed shower curtain. "Perhaps we should talk about why this is happening—"

"No!" Mei said sharply. "I mean—" Her voice softened. "Nah! It's okay."

"You are a woman now . . . ," her mother said.

Mei cringed. She stuffed both paws in her mouth and played along, pretending to listen intently. "Mmm-hmm!"

". . . and your body is starting to change," Ming continued.

"Mmmhhh." Mei wished her mother would stop talking.

"It's nothing to be embarrassed about!"

Finally, Mei couldn't take it. "MOM!" Mei said. "PLEASE!"

But her mother wouldn't be quiet. "You are now a beautiful, strong flower—" She reached for the curtain.

Mei stared at her mother's hand, gripping the curtain. She braced herself. "No, no, no, no, no, no!"

Ming began to draw the curtain open as she continued. "—a strong flower who must protect her delicate petals and clean them regularly—"

Suddenly, the sound of a shrieking smoke alarm pierced the air from the kitchen just as Ming threw the curtain wide open. But Ming wasn't looking at Mei. She was looking toward the bathroom door.

"Uh, Ming?" Jin called. "Ming!"

"My porridge!" Ming exclaimed. She let go of the curtain and rushed out. "Jin! JIN!"

From the hallway, Ming spotted smoke filling the hall. Jin ran across the kitchen, holding a fire extinguisher above his head. He was still shouting for her.

Ming hurried to the kitchen.

While Mei's parents were distracted, Mei sprinted for her bedroom.

"Jin!" Ming said. "Open a window!"

Mei made it to her room and slammed the door. Her ungainly body knocked things over as she leaped into her bed. She slipped under the covers. "I'll just go to sleep," Mei said to herself, out of breath. "And when I wake up . . . this will be all over."

Some bed slats broke.

Mei took a deep breath. *Just go to sleep.* Then another deep breath. *Calm down.*

On the third breath, her panda ears suddenly *poof*ed away. Mei felt her head with her paws. "What the?"

She got out of bed and stared at herself in the mirror. She took another deep, calming breath. Another *poof*! Her tail disappeared. *Whoa.*

The wheels in Mei's head began to turn. She searched her room and grabbed two hairbrushes from her dresser. She ran them over her head and face. *Ahhh.* It felt so good. She closed her eyes and took two more deep, slow breaths. *That's it. Be calm.*

Poomph! A pink cloud enveloped her. When it dissipated, Mei looked down at her human self. Still holding the hairbrushes, she pumped her fists with joy. "Yes!"

Phwoom!

She was back to being a red panda again.

"*No!*" Mei tossed the brushes to the floor.

Wait a second. Maybe . . .

Mei closed her eyes, put her paws together as if in a meditative yogalike prayer, and took more deep breaths in between words. "I'm calm . . . zen . . ."

Phwoof!

She was a girl again.

Mei was careful not to get too excited—she didn't want to trigger another panda moment. She did a quiet, mini fist pump. *Yes.*

She went to the mirror to make sure everything was in order. She looked like her regular self, except . . . *her hair.* It was bright red.

"Okay," Mei said, remembering to keep her cool. "No biggie." She slowly backed up to her broken bed and gingerly sat on the edge of it. "You'll figure this out, Lee. Just be the calm . . . mature . . . adult you totally are."

Her bed collapsed even farther toward the floor. She ignored it. "You got this."

Chapter 5

Wearing a knit hat to cover her red hair, Mei sat in the passenger seat of their car with her backpack in her lap while her mother pulled up to school. Mei watched the students file into the building.

"I know it feels strange," Ming said, thinking of her blossoming daughter. "But I promise, nobody will notice a thing."

Mei looked at her mother, barely moving her head. She spoke in a super-calm, almost robotic tone. The last thing she needed was to get excited and make an appearance at school as an animal. "Thank you for your concern, Mother. But I'll be fine."

Ming grabbed a brown bag from the backseat and placed it in Mei's backpack. "Well . . . here's your lunch. I packed extra snacks, and herbal tea. For cramps. It helps relax your—"

"I got it," Mei said. "Thank you. Bye." Mei hustled out of the car and toward the school. She looked back and saw her mother parked at the curb, staring at her. Mei gave her mom a wan smile and managed two thumbs up. Ming waved and then pulled away.

Mei reached the top of the steps, paused for a moment, and opened the door.

To everyone else, it was just a normal school day. Mei tried to look casual as students talked in the hall and got their things out of their lockers for class. Mei spotted Miriam, Priya, and Abby in their usual spots. She walked down the hall like nothing was wrong. *Remain calm.*

Her friends saw her right away. "Hey, Mei!" Miriam said.

"Hey, girlfriends," Mei said, practically like an android. "What is up?" Mei kept walking. Puzzled, her friends fell in line with her.

"Uh," Miriam said, noticing Mei's hat. "What's with the tuque?"

"Bad hair day," Mei said sheepishly.

Abby caught a whiff of her and frowned. "Did you, like, work out this morning?

"I got you, girl," Priya said, brandishing a deodorant stick. Mei grabbed it and put some on. Then, for good measure, she swiped her neck and face with it, too. She handed the deodorant back to Priya.

"Mei," Miriam said seriously. "We gotta talk."

"Okay," Mei said.

"Tyler's been telling everyone about the Daisy Mart," Miriam began.

Mei struggled to remain composed. "What?"

"He said your mom went nuts," Abby added.

"And that you're kind of a perv," Priya finished.

Mei gritted her teeth. "I'm not a—" She caught herself and stopped in the middle of the hall. She let out a long breath. *Don't. Get. Worked. Up.* "Tyler is an insecure jerkwad," she said coolly. "Words were exchanged. Slightly uncomfortable secrets were revealed. End . . . of—" A handsome dark-haired boy crossed Mei's path. Mei stopped and turned to face him. As if in slow motion, Mei watched the boy toss his beautiful hair out of his eyes. "—story," she managed, breathless.

"Uh . . . Mei?" Miriam said.

Mei gasped.

"Why are you staring at Carter Murphy-Mayhew?" Miriam said.

Mei blushed. "I wasn't!" She pushed Carter out of her mind and then spotted evil Tyler across the hall by a classroom door. Was that—? Was he taping a copy of her Devon merman drawing to the door? "No!" she shouted. Her heart started pounding. Then she noticed another drawing of Devon taped to a nearby locker. Mei ripped the drawing down and tossed it to the floor. She gritted her teeth, seething as she stared at Tyler. *How . . . dare . . . he!*

"Ugh," Miriam said. "Tyler keeps putting them up." She yelled at him. "Knock it off!"

"Not funny, Tyler!" Abby shouted.

Tyler turned to look at them, laughing. "Oh, Devon!"

he teased. "My precious manly man!" He turned, hugged himself, and made smooching sounds as though he were making out with someone.

Mei's friends formed a wall between Mei and Tyler. "You're such a loser, Tyler!" Miriam yelled. "Literally, go away!"

"I banish you," Priya said. "Begone, braceface."

Tyler wouldn't stop cackling. "Take me to your underwater palace!" He made more kissing sounds.

Mei scanned the hall. The pictures she had drawn were *everywhere*.

Abby began cursing in Korean.

Mei's temperature rose. "I'm gonna KILL HIM!" she growled.

POOF!

One of Mei's hands became a panda fist. Mei somehow managed to force it away, but then her fluffy tail shot out.

Mei gasped. She looked at her friends, whose backs were turned to her. No one had noticed anything.

"Leave her alone," Miriam said.

"Let's go," Abby said. "You wanna piece of me, huh? Come here!"

Mei tried to make her tail go away, but it was no use. She frantically tried to stuff it into her jeans. It was pointless.

Tyler started to move away from the girls. "Smell ya later, dorks!"

"You better run!" Abby said.

"Yep," Miriam said, "that's what I thought. Get outta here, dude!"

"Yeah," Abby said.

Mei backed away from her friends. She kept her tail down with one hand and waved to her friends with the other. "Gotta go! See ya at lunch!" She lunged for her math class door nearby.

Inside the classroom, Mei checked for her tail. It was gone! She sighed with relief, slid behind her desk, and unzipped her backpack. She chugged the herbal tea her mother had packed for her. Then she put her head on her desk and tried to catch her breath. As she inhaled, she could hear Miriam taking the seat next to her.

"What's with *her*?" said a nosy girl behind them.

Miriam turned in her seat. "What's with your face?" she snapped back. She leaned into Mei and kept her voice low. "What *is* with you? You're being weird."

Mei put on a smile. "I'm just . . . really excited about math."

Mr. Kieslowski stood at the front of the class, pointing to the chalkboard. "All right, guys. The quadratic formula . . ."

The rest of the class groaned, but Mei took out her notebook and twirled her fuzzy pen.

"Let the fun begin!" Mr. K said. "Now, who can tell me how the formula begins?"

As Mr. K conducted the lesson, Miriam wrote a note and slipped it to Mei: *U SURE U'R OK?*

Mei quickly wrote back: *Yup! All good!*

Mr. K droned on about Xs, plusses, and minuses.

Miriam passed another note.

Mei passed it back without reading it.

Miriam tapped the note, insistent.

Mei reluctantly read it.

YOUR MOM IS OUTSIDE.

Mei's eyes bulged. She slowly turned to stare through the classroom windows. There she was—her mother, wearing dark sunglasses, peeking out from behind a tree.

Mei gasped. She sank in her chair and tried to pretend she was invisible. Her heart raced. *No, no, no, this isn't happening. . . .*

Mei continued to watch her mom from the corner of her eye. Now the school security guard was talking to her. Mei strained to hear what they were saying. Their voices were muffled but still audible.

"Uh, ma'am, hi!" the security guard said.

"My child goes to this school," Ming said.

"Why don't you come to the front office?" the guard said. "I'm sure there's someone who can assist you."

Some of the kids in Mei's class noticed the conversation happening outside and turned to look. Then Mei watched in horror as Ming kicked the guard in the shin. The guard stumbled backward.

"Ow!" he cried.

"I pay my taxes," Ming said.

Miriam got up from her chair and joined other classmates who were now gathering by the window.

Mei wilted in her seat. She couldn't look.

"All right, all right," Mr. K said. "Settle down, little goblins." He joined the class at the window. His jaw dropped as he watched the scene outside unfold. The security guard and Mei's mother were getting into a full-on fight. "Whoa."

Mei tried to keep breathing as all the kids pressed themselves against the glass to get a better look.

No, please, no! Mei said to herself. She cowered at her desk. If anyone could literally die from embarrassment, Mei was on the verge.

Then Mei heard her mother calling for her. "Mei-Mei! MEI-MEI! Call someone!"

Ming ran toward the window, but the guard blocked her. "Mei-Mei," Ming called, "tell him it's me!"

Mei's class burst into laughter as the guard tried to drag Ming away.

Ming lunged toward Mei's classroom again. "Mei-Mei!" she called. "Tell him it's Mommmmeeeee!" She whipped out a box of pads and thrust it high into the air. "Tell them you forgot your pads!"

The class and Mr. K recoiled in shock and embarrassment.

Mei's eyes widened. She was mortified. *"Agggggghhhhhh!"* She couldn't take it anymore.

Phwwwwwooopmh! A huge cloud of pink smoke filled the room.

Mei had just exploded into her worst nightmare.

Again.

The giant red panda was back.

Chapter 6

Kids screamed in the haze. Mei looked around. Miriam and her classmates were too busy choking on the smoke to notice her giant panda self in the room.

Mei saw her mother outside, struggling with the guard. They locked eyes.

Oh, no. Her mother had seen her.

Ming gaped at her daughter's huge red panda form.

Mr. K opened a window and smoke billowed out. Mei panicked and ran from the classroom.

In the chaos, the guard let Ming go. Ming ran to the building and climbed through the window. "Mei-Mei, come back!"

Mei skidded into the hall. She knocked over trash cans and a utility cart as she sprinted for the girls' room. She accidentally barreled into two band kids on the way. A trombone went flying. The kids fell to the floor without even knowing what had hit them. Mei dashed into the restroom and wedged the edge of a trash can underneath the door handle. Just then, Stacy Frick came out of a stall. She looked up at Mei and froze.

"O-M—" she began.

Mei covered Stacy's face with her enormous paw, muffling her voice. She gently pushed Stacy back into the stall. The trash can at the door shook as a student in the hall banged on the door to get in.

"Hey!" she said. "I gotta go! Open up!"

Mei jolted back into action and jammed her huge body through a window. She fell outside in a heap, rolled to her feet, and ran past another classroom window. On the other side of the glass was Ming!

Ming spotted Mei and changed direction to follow her.

Mei shoved a gate open and raced past the entrance of the school just as Ming burst through the front doors. She waved frantically at her daughter.

"Mei-Mei! Stop!" she called.

But Mei was too far away to hear her. Ming ran to her car and peeled out of the lot. She called her husband on her phone as she drove. "Jin, JIN! Get home now! There's been an emergency."

"Is it the woman thing?" Jin said.

"NO!" Ming replied. "Another one!"

Mei raced down an alleyway. When she emerged, she ran headlong into a man and a woman enjoying a stroll.

"It's a monster!" the man said.

The woman screamed, "Run!"

Mei turned and ran in the opposite direction. She stumbled, flailing, and crashed into the patio furniture of an outdoor café. She knocked a man wearing headphones out of his chair.

Mei veered into a filthy narrow alley. She tried to squeeze through, but she was too fat. She had to squirm and wiggle her way through. She finally popped out the other side and fell to the ground. She gagged, grossed out from the garbage and filth smeared all over her fur. *"Bleaggh!"*

Mei hurried past a storefront, then stopped to see her disgusting reflection in the window. As she removed garbage stuck to her fur, her focus shifted to inside the store, where Devon was reading a magazine. Suddenly, she got *that feeling* again, the same one she'd had in her room and when she'd seen Carter Murphy-Mayhew. Mei slapped her face—*STOP IT.* She bolted just as Devon turned, unaware of who or what had just been outside the store.

Mei peeked out from behind a building, then darted down the sidewalk. Attempting to hide her enormous bulk from a passing skateboarder, she hid beside a parked delivery van, not realizing that she was in the middle of the street.

A car horn honked. Tires screeched. A green sedan stopped inches away from her. For a split second, Mei and the driver stared at each other. The driver screamed. Cars piled up behind them. Mei jumped onto the roof of a car and then she leaped onto a fire escape nearby. She scrambled up the ladder. As she climbed, the top end of the fire escape came loose from the building. Agh! Mei clung to the ladder as the entire escape fell backward. She jumped off the ladder and landed on a sign anchored to another building. Mei used the sign like a stepstool as she clung to the roof's edge, but the sign quickly gave way beneath her weight and crashed to the ground.

Ming's car pulled up and screeched to a halt. Ming looked up and gasped as she saw a flash of red fur scrambling onto a rooftop.

"Oh, Mei-Mei!" Ming jumped out of the car, took off her heels, and dashed after her daughter, barefoot. "Mei-Mei!"

Mei raced across roof after roof, terrified. *Gotta get home, gotta hide!* She leaped across the gulf between two buildings just as some kids playing basketball looked up to see her giant shadow pass over them.

On the ground, Ming ran through the paused basketball game as the dumbfounded kids wondered what they had just seen.

Ming called after her daughter again. "Mei-Mei!"

Mei was too far ahead. She spotted the roof of the temple straight in front of her. *Home, home, home.* She pushed off with her giant feet and flew through the air. Mr. Gao, who was watering plants on his rooftop garden, looked up to see Panda Mei soaring overhead. He stopped, stunned.

Mei sailed toward the temple wall. She took in a breath,

anticipating that she'd clear the wall, but came up short. She belly-flopped onto the wall and slid to the ground outside the gate. *Yow!* In pain, Mei flung open the gates and barreled into the courtyard, crying. She dashed for her house, breaking pottery and knocking things over along the way.

When Ming arrived inside the temple gates, she could barely catch her breath. "Mei-Mei!" She sprinted through the courtyard. The security gate that led to their house was hanging open. Shards of pottery were all over the ground. The front door to their home was standing open.

Ming went inside and saw the destruction left in Mei's wake. Giant dirty paw prints were everywhere, along with clumps of Mei's fur.

Ming hurried toward Mei's bedroom, where Mei was curled up in a ball under her comforter, blubbering nonsensically.

Mei heard her mom calling for her. She reached for her hairbrushes and frantically brushed her cheeks with long strokes, trying to calm down. "Don't look at me!" Mei said. "Stay back!"

"Sweetie," Ming said as she entered the room. "It's okay—Mommy's here!" Ming kneeled next to her daughter and gingerly reached out to comfort her.

"What's happening to me?" Mei wailed.

Jin suddenly ran in, out of breath. "What is it? Wha—"

He gasped when he saw Ming . . . and the ginormous shape in Mei's bed. "It's happened already?"

Mei stopped brushing her cheeks. *Happened already?* Mei turned to stare at her parents. "What did you say?"

Ming avoided Jin's gaze.

Jin placed a hand on his wife's shoulder. "Ming, it's time."

The temple door opened. Light spilled onto the tapestry of Sun Yee above the altar. Ming, Jin, and Mei, still in panda form, entered the room. Ming lifted the tapestry and opened a secret compartment built into the wall. She took out a small ancient chest. Mei stood beside her dad. She stared at the chest in her mother's hands.

What do my parents know about my . . . condition?

Ming set the box down on the altar, lifted the lid, and pulled out a scroll. "As you know, our ancestor Sun Yee had a mystical connection with red pandas."

Ming unrolled the scroll to reveal images of Sun Yee as a young woman turning into a red panda.

"In fact," Ming continued, "she loved them so much that she asked the gods to turn her into one. It was wartime. The men were all gone. Sun Yee was desperate for a way to protect herself and her daughters. Then one night, during a red moon, the gods granted her wish. They gave her the ability to harness her emotions to transform into a powerful, mystical beast. She was able to fend off bandits, protect her village, and save her family from ruin."

Mei listened, wide-eyed, taking it all in. The pictures on the scroll were ominous, but heroic, too.

Ming continued. "Sun Yee passed this gift to her daughters when they came of age. And they passed it to theirs. But over time, our family chose to come to a new world. And what was once a blessing became an inconvenience."

An inconvenience? Mei thought. Her mind went to what she had just gone through, and she spoke to Sun Yee in the portrait. "Are . . . you . . . SERIOUS?" She lunged at the tapestry.

Ming and Jin tried to hold her back. "Mei-Mei, NO!" Ming said.

"It's a curse!" Mei shouted at the woven image of her ancestor. "You cursed us! IT'S ALL YOUR FAULT!"

"She meant it as a blessing," Ming said, struggling to hold her daughter back.

Mei's sharp claws slashed through the air. The ground rumbled. The altar shook, sending objects in the room flying. The lanterns hanging from the ceiling swayed from the commotion.

Ming and Jin pushed with all their might to keep Panda Mei away from the altar.

"Mei-Mei! Listen to me! There's a cure!" exclaimed Ming.

Mei paused for a moment to consider what her mother had said. "Really? How do you know?"

"Because it happened to me," said Ming.

"Why didn't you warn me?" Mei asked.

"I thought I had more time!" Ming said. "You're just a child. I thought if I watched you like a hawk and never left your side, I'd see the signs, be able to prepare!" Ming paused and took a breath. "But it's going to be fine. I overcame it, and you will, too."

She took off the necklace she was wearing and showed Mei the jade pendant hanging off the chain. "On the next red moon, you'll undergo a ritual that will seal your red panda spirit into one of these. And then you'll be cured. For good. Just like me."

Mei had seen the pendant all her life, but now she looked at it with new eyes. The pendant glowed as if something alive was trapped within.

Ming put her necklace back on and stepped closer to Mei.

"Any strong emotion will release the panda," Ming warned. "And the more you release it, the more difficult the ritual will be. There is a darkness to the panda, Mei-Mei. You only have one chance to banish it, and you cannot fail. Otherwise . . . you will never be free."

Mei gulped. *Never be free?*

Jin scrutinized a Chinese calendar hanging on the wall.

He flipped it to May. "Let's see. . . . The next red moon will be the twenty-fifth."

"That's a whole month away," Mei said.

Ming gently took Mei's paw in her hands. "Don't worry. We'll wait it out together. And I'll be with you every step of the way."

When Mei, no longer a panda, returned to her room to sleep for the night, her parents had moved all her belongings and furniture out of the room. The only thing left was her mattress, with her bedding, on the floor. Mei sat on the mattress.

"Hmm," Jin said, looking around. "Not bad."

Mei sighed. Her room looked like a cell that wasn't even padded. She already missed her books, her motivational posters, and her swivel chair! She tried to hold back the tears.

Ming kneeled beside Mei. From the other side of the mattress, Jin handed Mei her pug plushie.

"I saved Wilfred," Jin said.

Mei gasped at the sight of her favorite childhood toy. "Thanks, Dad."

Mei hugged Wilfred to her chest, grateful. She took off her glasses, handed them to Jin, and lay back on her mattress.

Ming tucked Mei in with a reassuring smile. "It's only temporary, Mei-Mei," she said, referring to her room. "This way we won't worry about any more accidents." She kissed her daughter good night, said "Sleep tight," and left the room.

Jin lingered in the doorway. He looked down at Mei. "Red is a lucky color." He turned and closed the door.

Mei rolled onto her back. She took a deep breath and studied her hands in the moonlight. They looked normal. *Human.* Then she heard the faint murmur of her parents' voices.

"This is awful . . . ," Ming said. "What are we going to do?"

"Don't worry," Jin replied. "We'll get through this."

"Did you see how she was in the temple?" said Ming. "Her eyes . . ."

Mei caught her breath and started to cry. Waves of sadness crushed her. She *phwoomp*ed into a panda and sobbed quietly on her mattress.

Outside, the sky was dark with a full moon. Mei had gone from a perfect daughter to a disgusting feral creature in the blink of an eye. She curled into a tight ball, clutching Wilfred. She had *thirty* days until the red moon. How would she survive?

Chapter 7

A handwritten sign on the locked temple gates read *CLOSED! Due to Family Emergency.*

While Jin straightened the kitchen, Ming vacuumed the living room, trying to suck up the fur that Mei had left the day before. A loud thud rocked the house. Ming shut off the vacuum and listened. The sound was coming from Mei's room. *That must be Mei,* she thought. *Poor thing.* There was another thud. The house shook, and Ming lunged to catch a framed photo of young Mei falling from the wall. Ming hung the photo back up and sighed with relief. She looked to Jin, who seemed to be thinking the same thing. They both knew. Their daughter needed time to adjust. Having a panda problem could be more than upsetting.

More thuds.

In her bedroom, Mei tried to wrestle her panda self into submission. She stood in the middle of her room, a girl from the neck down and a giant panda head from the neck up. She rammed her panda head right into the wall. *Poof!*

She was now a girl from the waist up but a panda from the waist down.

She yanked on her own tail and somersaulted away from the wall. She slammed a panda arm against the floor, which then turned into her normal girl arm. Then she yanked her panda ears into girl ears. Her transformation only half complete, she collapsed.

"Please . . . just . . . go away . . . ," she moaned.

Suddenly, she *poof*ed into a whole panda. "Ahhhh! No! Why, why?" She squeezed her eyes shut. She could barely stand to see herself.

Tap, tap, tap.

Mei cracked open one eye and looked toward her window.

"Mei?" Miriam said in a loud whisper. "It's us! Open up!"

No! Still a panda, Mei leaped to her feet and closed the curtains before her friends could see her. "Guys, what are you doing?" she whispered, panicked. "Go away."

Outside, Miriam, Priya, and Abby stared at Mei's curtained window, concerned. They hadn't heard Mei at all.

"Are you okay?" Priya said. "Tap if you can hear us!"

"One for yes," Abby said. "Two for no!"

"We were so worried!" Miriam said. "We thought you had died from embarrassment."

"You need more pads?" Priya said. "I brought extra."

Abby whipped out a flyer for 4*Town and held it up to the window. "Forget that—4*Town's coming to Toronto!"

"What?" Mei said as she yanked the curtain open without thinking.

The girls started at Panda Mei through the window. Their jaws dropped. They screamed in unison. "AHHHHH!"

"Shhh! Shhhhh!" Mei opened the window and pulled them into her room. She hugged them into her furry chest, muffling their screams.

"It's all right!" Mei said. "Everybody, it's just me! Shut up! It's okay, it's me. It's Mei! Calm down. I'm gonna let go, and you're gonna be chill . . . got that?"

Her friends stopped screaming. They stared up at her, wide-eyed, and nodded.

"CHILL," Mei commanded.

She carefully let them go. They stared at her in a hushed awe.

Miriam finally found her voice. "Mei?"

"Are you a werewolf?" Priya blurted.

"No!" Mei said. "What?"

To Abby, this was a dream come true! "SHE'S A RED PANDA."

"Sick," Priya said, but she meant it in a good way.

"You're so fluffy!" Abby buried her face in Mei's furry belly. "YOU'RE SO FLUFFY!" she said again.

"I've always wanted a tail," Priya said.

"Priya, Abby, quit it," Miriam said. "Mei . . . what the heck happened?"

Mei tried to put on a brave front. "It's just some . . . you know, inconvenient, uh . . . genetic thingy I got from my mom. . . . I mean . . . it'll go away, eventually . . . maybe." She broke down, sobbing. Her friends rushed forward.

"Aw, Mei!" Miriam said.

"I hate this," Mei said. "I'm slobby, I'm smelly, my mom won't even look at me. And now 4*Town? When are they coming?"

"May eighteenth!" Abby said. "They just announced it!"

"The eighteenth?" Mei wept some more. "There's no way this'll be gone by then! Just go. . . ." She waved her friends away. "Go become women without me."

"Mei, it's gonna be okay," Miriam said.

"No, it's not," Mei retorted. "I'm a freak. Just leave me alone." She curled up on the floor, snatched Wilfred from her mattress, and cuddled him.

Miriam, Priya, and Abby stood quietly for a moment.

Then Miriam began to beatbox. "Boots 'n' cats, boots 'n' cats . . ."

Abby picked up the cue and started, too. "Mm. Yeah. Mm. Let's go. Mm. Yeah . . ."

Priya joined in. Then all three of them broke out into an a cappella version of Mei's favorite 4*Town hit, complete with choreography.

When the song ended, the girls cheered.

"Yeah!" Miriam said.

"Go, Mei!" Priya added.

"Woo!" yelled Abby.

"Thanks, guys," Mei said, touched. "You're the best."

Her friends looked up at her. "Aww," Miriam said. "We love you, Mei."

"You're our girl," Priya agreed.

"No matter what." Miriam said. "Panda or no panda."

Mei hugged her friends, overwhelmed with gratitude. She let out a long breath. Then she *phoompf*ed backed into a girl. Her besties looked at her, amazed.

Miriam gasped.

"Whoa, Mei!" Priya said.

"You're you!" Miriam stared at Mei's red hair. "And you look amazing!"

"Red looks so good on you," Priya said.

Abby shoved Miriam out of the way and approached Mei. "Aw, is it gone?"

"For now," Mei said. "But if I get too excited, it'll come right ba—"

Abby pinched her cheek.

"OW!" Mei said, "Abby, what the heck?" She paused. "Huh, something feels . . . *different.*"

Mei tapped her own arm. "Abby, hit me."

Abby looked at Mei's arm, then punched her in the face.

Mei went down, then popped back up, dazed. Her cheek hurt. But she was thrilled. She had remained human! "Omigosh! I stayed calm. Something about you guys, like, neutralizes the panda!"

Miriam and Abby celebrated with Mei. "It's our love!" cried Miriam.

"We're like a warm and fuzzy blanket," Priya said.

"Yeah," said Abby, somewhat disappointed.

Mei gasped. "This means . . . I can have my room back!" She gasped again. "I can have my *life* back!"

"No, even better," Miriam said, "you can come with us to 4*Town!"

"Huh?" Mei said.

"This could be our only chance to see them together," Miriam went on. "We're all asking our parents tonight!"

"We're making our stand," Priya said.

"Yeah," Abby said. "You in or out?"

"But I can't ask my mom," Mei replied. "I'm a furry, ticking time bomb!"

"Of awesomeness," Miriam added. "And now you can control it. So just *prove* it to her, and she's got to let you go."

Mei hesitated. This was huge. *Can I convince my mother?*

Just then, Mei heard that very person calling for her. "Mei-Mei?"

Mei stared at her friends. "You guys better go!"

Miriam didn't move. "But—"

"No buts, Mir," Mei said, hustling everyone out the window. "My mom already doesn't like you."

"Wait," Miriam said, turning back to look at her. "She doesn't?"

Mei ignored her question. "I'll call you, I promise!"

"Hang in there, girl," Abby said.

"We love you, Mei," Priya said.

Mei shut the window and pulled the curtains closed, her mind racing. Just then, Ming opened the door. She looked tired. "Everything okay? I thought I heard—"

"Mom," Mei interrupted. She couldn't wait to share her new discovery. "I think I've made a breakthrough."

Chapter 8

Mei sat at the kitchen table, completely focused, her gaze trained on her parents. Seated opposite Mei, her parents watched her, apprehensive. Jin held photos in his hands.

"Ready," Mei said.

Jin flipped through the photos. He showed one to Mei.

"Deforestation," Ming said.

Mei looked at the picture of downed trees and imagined the thousands of creatures that had just lost their homes. They hadn't done anything to deserve that! Yet she maintained control of her feelings. She said nothing, did nothing.

Satisfied, Jin showed his daughter another photo.

"Sad orangutan," Ming said.

Mei held back from any outward expression, even though she was experiencing a tiny death inside.

Next . . .

Ming called out the picture. "Your second-place spelling bee trophy."

Mei trembled. She squeezed her eyes shut. The memory

still burned strong, as though it had happened yesterday. She quickly imagined Miriam, Priya, and Abby reassuring her and supporting her.

"The important thing is you tried," Miriam had said.

"You spelled your little butt off," Priya had said.

"First place in our hearts," Abby had added.

Mei opened her eyes, inhaled, then exhaled. "What . . . a . . . shame."

Ming nodded at Jin. It was time for the big guns.

Jin gulped.

Mei watched her father get up from the table. He returned with a large cardboard box that had been folded shut.

Jin set the box on the table.

Her parents slowly backed away.

Mei hesitantly opened the box. Inside, a whole litter of adorable kittens stared up at her with enormous imploring eyes.

Mei gasped. She broke into a sweat. "So . . . cute . . . ," she said weakly.

Mei clutched the edge of her skirt to keep herself from petting the soft kittens. The little creatures clambered out of the box, then crawled all over her, mewing and purring.

"Must . . . resist!" Mei closed her eyes again. The kittens became Miriam, Priya, and Abby, and they were hugging her. They all sighed, feeling relaxed.

Mei looked at her friends and smiled, feeling safe and

loved. "We love you, girl," they said in unison. "Panda or no panda," Miriam added.

Another group hug.

Mei inhaled, then exhaled, and returned once more to the situation at hand, her eyes still closed. Covered in kittens, Mei opened her eyes, and . . .

. . . stayed human.

"How . . . adorable," she said calmly.

Her parents stared at Mei, shocked. One of the kittens mewed.

"Mei!" said Jin.

"How is this possible?" Ming said. "What happened to your panda?"

"It's easy," Mei explained. "When I start to get emotional, all I do is imagine the people I love most in the whole world—" She thought of her friends.

Ming leaned forward, touched.

Mei stopped herself. "—which is you guys." She lied.

"Oh, Mei-Mei!" her mother said, melting. She went in for a hug.

Mei had her mother right where she wanted her. *Could it be?* Mei's eyes went wide. *Could this really be working?*

"So now that that's settled," said Mei, "I just have one teeny tiny favor to ask. . . ."

Ming and Jin sat on the Lee family couch.

"No," Ming said sternly. "Absolutely not!"

Mei was kneeling in front of her parents and breathing hard in a blazer with an unlit sparkler in each hand. Behind her, a white sheet hung on the wall where a projector displayed an image of Mei's presentation, entitled "4*Town: Why I Must Go." Below the title, Mei had inserted pictures of the world's greatest child musician prodigies: Chopin, Mozart, Beethoven, and, of course, the 4*Town members, front and center.

"But this is once in a lifetime!" Mei said.

Jin studied a 4*Town brochure he now held.

"Mei-Mei," said Ming, "it's one thing to stay calm at home or school, but a concert? You'll get whipped into a frenzy, and panda all over the place."

"I won't, I won't," Mei promised. "You saw me keep it in."

"Ming," Jin said, "maybe we should trust her—"

Ming pointed at the pictures of the 4*Town boys. "It's them I don't trust. Look at those glittery delinquents with their . . . *gyrations*! Why on earth do you want to go so badly?"

Mei took a moment to think hard about the question. She instantly saw herself at the stadium dancing with her friends while 4*Town was onstage. They downed soda while 4*Town cheered, "Chug! Chug! Chug! Chug!"

Abby burped. Robaire suddenly came out of nowhere and proposed to Mei on one knee. The rest of 4*Town seemed moved while Mei's friends and the crowd celebrated the joyous couple. Then Mei and her friends were lifted into the air by each of their favorite 4*Town members.

Suddenly, Mei snapped back to reality. "Like I said," she told her mother. "I just want to broaden my musical horizons."

Ming let out a disgusted sigh. "This isn't music. This is *filth*, and it's not worth jeopardizing your life over. Right, Jin?"

"Uh . . ."

"See?" Ming said. "Your father agrees. No concert. And that's final."

Mei felt a flash of anger zip through her. She took a deep breath. She needed to hold tight to her humanness. "Okay, well, thanks for listening. G'night." She took down her presentation and grabbed the bust of a famous composer that she had used for her talk. Then she narrowed her eyes at her mother just before she scooted out of the room.

Ming and Jin watched her go. They heard Mei's bedroom door slam shut.

"What was that?" Ming said.

Jin opened his mouth to say something, but Ming wagged a finger in his face. "Am I the only one who sees the danger here? There's no way she could keep her panda in! And two hundred dollars? For what? Who do they think they are, Celine Dion?"

Jin sighed. The phone rang and he got up to answer it. "Wei? Hold on."

"I saw that look!" Ming said to herself from the couch. "Where does she get that from? Treating her own mother like that." She flopped back into the seat cushions and stretched out.

"Ming? It's your mother," said Jin.

Ming sat bolt upright. "I'm not here!"

Jin held the phone out to Ming. She grudgingly took it and forced a smile.

"Mother!" she said brightly. "Hello."

Mei's grandmother was calling from her glitzy apartment, where she was watching the news. "Toronto residents were terrorized by a mysterious beast," the reporter had said. "Witnesses described it as an 'obese, sunburned bear.'"

"How's everything in Florida?" Ming said. Her mother had her on speakerphone.

Grandma, who had been sitting at her makeup vanity, wrapped her elegant hand around a makeup brush as she readied herself for a night out. "Ming, I know about Mei-Mei," she said as she applied blush to her cheeks. A jade bracelet dangled from her wrist.

"I was just about to call you," Ming said. "But everything's fine. I'm going to handle the ritual on my own—"

Grandma scoffed. "The way you handled Mei-Mei being on the news?" She applied lipstick to her delicate mouth and pursed her lips.

"No one knows anything," Ming said. "They barely saw her!"

"I'm on my way," Grandma said. "With reinforcements."

"No, I can handle it," Ming insisted. "I can—"

Grandma hung up.

Ming's eyes bulged. *My mother is coming?*

She dropped the phone to the floor.

Chapter 9

Outside on the school grounds, Mei and her classmates played dodgeball in their gym uniforms.

"Eyes on the ball!" Mr. K shouted. Balls flew everywhere. "Be water. Be—"

A boy got hit and was knocked to the asphalt.

"Guys!" Mr. K said. *"Eyes on the balls!"*

Another boy screamed in agony from the impact.

But dodgeball was the last thing Mei and her friends had been thinking about. Mei filled in Miriam, Abby, and Priya about the previous night's debacle. "The presentation was bomb-dot-com!" Mei said as a ball flew past. "I cited all my sources. I had SPARKLERS." She caught a ball and threw it at no one in particular. "She still said no."

A ball whizzed by Priya. "My parents said I could go when I'm thirty," she lamented.

"Mine called it stripper music!" Abby said, deflecting an incoming ball.

"Mine said yes," Miriam remarked, *"but* I have to buy

the ticket." Miriam ducked as a ball flew overhead. "Who the heck's got that kind of cash?"

A ball bounced toward Mei. She caught it. "I know my mom's worried, but sometimes she's just so . . . so . . ."

"Wacko?" Miriam offered. She pointed across the street. There was Ming, in her car, watching them. The school security guard rushed toward the vehicle, waving his arms. "Ma'am, please! Sorry, Mrs. Lee! I see you!"

Ming drove off, tires screeching.

Mei heard someone laughing hysterically. She turned to see Tyler talking to another boy, hundreds of feet way. Tyler cackled some more. "Little mama's girl! No wonder Mei's such a loser."

Mei gripped the ball in her hands. She could feel her face heating up.

Tyler kept laughing, further spiking her rage.

Poof! Her arm became a panda arm. She hurled the ball *hard.*

The ball zoomed toward Tyler.

"Ahhhh!" Tyler ducked, the ball grazing his hair. The ball crashed through a school window.

Mr. K blew his whistle. "Illegal throw! You're out, Lee!" He had not seen Mei's panda arm make an appearance.

"What?" Mei said. "But, Mr. K, he—"

Before Mei could finish her sentence, her friends hustled her off the court. "Mei, chill!" Miriam warned.

A couple of dodgeballers stared at Mei as she was dragged off, including Stacy Frick, the girl who had seen Mei in the bathroom. Her eyes narrowed. *She* had noticed Mei's arm. The furry appendage had looked very familiar.

Miriam, Abby, and Priya dragged Mei to the girl's room.

"Calm down, Mei," Miriam said, letting her go.

Mei was still panting with rage.

"Dude," Priya said, "Keep it together."

"I can't!" Mei said. "We need to see the concert. Why doesn't my mom get that? I never ask for anything! My whole life, I've been her perfect little Mei-Mei—temple duties, grades!"

"Violin," Abby volunteered.

"Tap-dancing," Priya added.

Now her friends were getting worked up, too.

"Yeah," Mei agreed. "We've been SO good. If they don't trust us anyway, then what's the point?"

Miriam was impressed. "Who *are* you?" She had never heard Mei talk like this. "I LOVE IT!"

"FIGHT THE POWER!" Abby declared.

Mei's eyes flashed. She took her friends' hands into hers. "Yeah! This isn't just our first concert. This is our first step into womanhood. And we have to do it together."

They nodded, deeply moved.

"I'm in, girl!" Miriam said. "We'll say it's a sleepover at my house!"

"The perfect crime!" Abby said.

"Yes," Mei agreed. "My mom will never know! Now we just gotta raise the money for tickets—c'mon, girls, think!"

They racked their brains.

"You know what will help me think?" Abby said. "A little panda." She rubbed her hands together.

"Abby," Mei said, annoyed.

"C'mon, Mei!" Abby begged. "It'll clear my mind! It's so freakin' cute!"

Mei let out a disgusted sound. "FINE." She opened her arms. Abby leaped into them.

Mei closed her eyes to concentrate and pictured herself floating underwater. In her mind's eye, she saw a flash of green scales. Then the beautiful merman Robaire swam up to her, reaching out his hand. *"Mon amour . . ."*

Phwoom! Mei panda'd up in a burst of pink smoke.

"Happy?" Mei said.

"Oh, yeah," Abby said, snuggling into Mei's furry arms like a baby.

Suddenly, a girl's voice rang out. "O.M.G."

Mei and her friends turned toward the door. Stacy Frick and two of her girlfriends were standing in the bathroom, staring at Mei.

Mei let go of Abby and dashed into a stall, slamming the door shut. "Go away!"

Mei's friends stood between the stall and Stacy Frick and her friends.

"That was YOU in the bathroom," Stacy said. "I didn't imagine it!"

"Yeah, you did!" Miriam said.

"Get lost, Stacy," Priya warned.

One of Stacy's friends spoke up. "But . . . she's like a magical . . . bear?"

"Red panda!" Mei and her friends corrected simultaneously.

Mei peeked over the top of the stall.

Stacy and her friends looked up at Mei, then at Mei's friends, then at each other.

Suddenly, the girls mobbed the stall door like they'd just caught a glimpse of 4*Town!

"Eeeee!" one of the girls squealed.

"Come out, please?" said another.

"You are the cutest thing EVER!" Stacy shrieked.

Amazed, Mei opened the door. "Wait, so . . . you . . . like the panda?"

"Like it?" one of the girls said. "I love it! I'll give you anything! Money!"

"My kidney!" offered the other.

"MY SOUL," Stacy said.

They started waving money at Mei as they clamored for more panda.

Mei and her friends stared at all the moolah. That was when Mei got the idea of the century.

Chapter 10

The next day, after school, Mei and her besties headed to an empty classroom with all their gear for their new project. As they crossed the hall, Mei removed the lens cap of her dad's videocam, powered it up, and flipped the viewfinder open.

Miriam stared at the camera lens. "Is it on?"

"Yo," Priya said into the camera. She was carrying Mei's backpack.

Abby gripped a bubble tea in one hand. "Wooo!"

They entered the classroom and Priya dumped a bunch of art supplies from Mei's backpack onto an empty table. "Let's go!" she said.

"Panda hustle! Money, money, money!" Miriam exclaimed.

Abby took a satisfying slurp from her tea for the camera's benefit, then helped Mei set up the classroom projector.

"4*Town, here we come!" Miriam said.

Mei pointed the camera at herself. "All right, troops,

listen up! Operation 4*Town Shakedown is about to commence!"

Abby turned on the projector and displayed Mei's drawing of the 4*Town boys with *Goal = $180* written in the center. The girls sat at their desks and clicked their pens.

Mei pointed to the next slide: a calendar showing the date of the concert on May 18 and the ritual on May 25. "The boys are comin' to Toronto. Our goal? Four tickets— that's eight hundred bucks." The projector clicked to a drawing of Ming. "Step one: neutralize the empress."

Mei had already taken care of this. She had told Ming she was joining Mathletes.

"Mathletes? Isn't it a little dangerous to join an after-school club now?" Ming had said.

"What's dangerous," Mei had replied, "is an academic record with a lack of extracurriculars!"

"Hmmm . . ." Ming had nodded and given her permission.

Mei flashed two fingers at the camera. It was time for Step Two. "Spread the word."

In history class, while students took a quiz, Abby passed a note to Stacy Frick. Stacy opened the note and saw a drawing of a camera, a red panda, and *Room 202* scribbled on it.

She immediately texted her friends: *OMG!!! PANDA PICS, ROOM 202!*

In the hallway not long afterward, a girl ran to join a line of curious kids outside a darkened classroom. Abby stood by the door at the head of the line, working it like a bouncer, letting groups of students inside one at a time.

In the classroom, human Mei waved hello to her newest group of fans. Behind her on the wall was a giant backdrop of the Canadian flag. Mei *phwoomph*ed into a panda, and everyone gasped. Then kids cheered as they rushed to give Panda Mei a big hug.

Step Three was about to begin: squeeze every last bit of cash out of her classmates.

Abby and Priya clicked on the lights, and Miriam snapped instant photos of Mei posing with various classmates.

A boy with his thumbs up. *Flash!*

Stacy Frick and a friend. *Flash!*

The basketball team. *Flash!*

With every picture, coins dropped into a lunch box. *Cha-ching!*

When it was time to tally things up, Mei and her besties gathered in their Mathletes classroom. They had made a hand-drawn thermometer on poster board. But instead of measuring degrees, it measured dollars, all the way up to eight hundred. They labeled it the Pandameter. With a marker, Miriam filled in the Pandameter to two hundred bucks! They jumped up and down with excitement.

"Yeah!" Abby cheered.

"Let's go!" cried Priya.

Each day after that, Mei and her friends continued to shake down the kids of Pearson Middle School. One day in the classroom, Mei posed with a group of students for another photo op. After the camera flashed, the kids left and Mei turned, crashing into Carter Murphy-Mayhew by accident. She fell on top of him.

"Oh!" Mei said with a sheepish laugh. She blushed and helped him up, then realized she had left a big paw print on his shirt. Carter looked down at his genuine Red Panda Girl autograph. He smiled at Mei and gave her a thumbs-up! Mei melted.

Back at the temple, Ming prayed before the altar of Sun Yee. She looked sadly at the empty cushion next to her. She missed her daughter, who hadn't shared dinner with her and Jin in days. Running the tours with only Jin for help had been challenging. But Ming knew as a parent that sacrifices had to be made. *For Mathletes,* she told herself. *For my daughter's academic future.*

As the days passed, Mei and her friends kicked their fundraising efforts up a notch. In the girls' restroom at school, Mei and her friends hawked Red Panda Girl T-shirts, stickers, posters, and more. Stacy Frick was their very first customer. She strutted out of the girls' room wearing a cute panda-ears headband and sporting a furry panda tail attached to the waistband of her skirt. Other kids gaped when they saw her and ran into the bathroom to get some RPG gear before it was going, going, gone!

More money fell into the lunch box. By May 8, less than two weeks from the 4*Town concert, the Pandameter was up to three hundred dollars! Even Tyler tried to get a photo with Red Panda Girl, but Abby stopped him when he got to the front of the line. She pointed at a sign behind her that read NO TYLERS. An eager girl behind Tyler shoved him out of the way. More cash was exchanged for panda merch. Before long, the Pandameter was up to four hundred dollars! They were halfway to their goal.

Ming felt sorry for Mei, working so hard every day. Ming also knew that Mei was nothing short of a miracle, keeping her panda under control the whole time. One day, she stopped by the school to deliver tasty baos made especially for her darling and the rest of the Mathletes team. Fortunately, Abby was posted at the fake Mathletes classroom door, counting their hard-earned cash, when she spotted Ming coming down the hall to make her delivery. Abby put away the money and gave Mei, Miriam, and Priya the signal. The girls scrambled inside to hide all the panda evidence. When Ming poked her head in the classroom, the girls had made it look like they were toiling away, solving complex math problems at their desks. They smiled innocently at Ming. Thankfully, the security guard shooed Mei's mother away—and snagged a bao before he followed her out.

After Mei's mom left, it was business as usual. A stack of cash was dropped into the overflowing lunch box. By

May 10, with only a week left before the concert, the Pandameter was up to six hundred smackaroos! In their fake Mathletes classroom, Mei and her friends played music to celebrate. Priya bobbed her head in time to the beat while Abby made it rain money. Mei was exuberant, triumphant! She decked herself out in merch and showed off some choreographed dancing. Then she *poof*ed toward the video camera which was recording and crashed into it. *Whoops!* The video turned to static.

When Mei arrived home that night, Ming and Jin were eating at the kitchen table. Ming brightened when she saw Mei come in and gave her a hug just before Mei breezed on to her room. Mei furtively shoved all her panda contraband under her bed: merch, money, photos, the calendar. She smiled. It wouldn't be long before her 4*Town dreams would come true.

The next day at school, the coach's whistle sounded on the asphalt basketball court. Various kids, decked out in panda merch, sat on the bleachers, watching the boys' team practice. Nearby, other middle schoolers hung out. A boy beatboxed while his friend tried out some dance moves, and another kid played a handheld video game while his friends cheered him on.

Mei, Miriam, Priya, and Abby sat in the bleachers. They were making Red Panda Girl charms with an arsenal of craft supplies. Mei hurriedly wrote on a clipboard. She was feeling a little anxious, trying to figure out what it would take to get that fourth concert ticket. The lunch box full of money was in her lap.

Miriam paused from her work for a moment to watch the basketball team. "Check out number twelve. He's got delts for days."

"Forget that," Abby said. "I need lunch. I'm starting to black out!" She collapsed against the bleachers.

Priya tried to get a piece of glitter off her hands. Her fingertips were so gluey. "I think I'm getting carpal tunnel."

"No pain, no gain, Priya!" Mei said. "C'mon! Chop-chop!" Mei opened the lunch box and re-counted the cash within. "Five, ten—"

"Girl, relax," Miriam said.

"Yeah," Abby said. "We're doing our best."

Mei's paws, ears, and tail *poof*ed out in frustration. She didn't even notice. "But it's not enough! The concert's this Saturday." Mei finished counting the money. "We're still a hundred short! I knew we shoulda charged more for photos. Stupid, stupid!"

Miriam scooted closer to Mei, worried that someone would notice her. "Mei, breathe!" she said, trying to calm her friend. They could get in trouble—or worse, Mei could wind up in an animal research lab for scientific study.

"It's in the bag!" Miriam reassured her.

"But—" Mei protested.

Miriam cut her off. "What's the point of getting to the concert if you're too exhausted to enjoy it?" She pointed

Mei's shoulders toward the basketball game. "Now take a break and help me appreciate some boys."

Maybe Miriam was right. She was getting a little over-worked. "Okay, okay, okay," Mei said. Her paws, ears, and tail *poof*ed away.

The girls looked out dreamily at the guys on the basketball court.

The boys waved at Mei. "Mei! What's up?" They started showing off to get her attention—they flexed, they posed.

Mei and her friends awkwardly flirted back.

"Woo!" Priya said.

"Lookin' good!" Miriam concurred.

"Nice calves," Abby added.

"Are you a triangle?" Mei said. "Cause you a-CUUUUTE!" She'd always wanted to try that one. The girls laughed.

A boy's voice floated up from beneath the bleachers. "You guys are so *weird.*"

The girls looked around, then spotted Tyler under the bleachers.

Talk about weird, Mei thought. *What is Tyler doing under the bleachers?*

"Hey!" Miriam said.

"Are you spying on us?" Mei asked.

"I wanna talk to you, Lee," Tyler said.

"Forget it," Mei said. Why would she dare talk to Tyler in such a hidden spot? People would think they had a thing or something. *Disgusting.* Wild *pandas* couldn't drag her.

"Fine," Tyler said. "Wonder if your mom knows her precious little Mei-Mei's been flauntin' the panda all over school?"

Mei and her friends gasped.

He wouldn't! Mei ran down the bleachers and headed underneath, straight for Tyler. Once she was hidden from view, she *phwoomph*ed into a panda. Could a large animal really be arrested for killing a despicable middle schooler? Mei's panda eyes were wild. "That's none of your business!" Mei seethed.

Tyler yelped and fell to the ground. Terrified, he whipped out his cell phone and held it up. "One more step, and I'm telling her everything! Now put that thing away and hear me out."

Ugh! Mei growled, then *poof*ed back into a girl. "What do you want?"

Tyler got up and dusted himself off. "I wanna throw a sick birthday party." He pulled a flyer from his pocket. "An *epic* one."

Mei's eyes scanned the info on the flyer. FRIDAY. 7 PM. TYLER'S BIRTHDAY. She raised an eyebrow and looked up to where her friends were watching through the bleachers. Miriam shrugged.

"It's *this* Friday," Tyler said. "If you're there, everyone will come. Simple as that."

Mei thought it over. "A party?" She tried to imagine herself as a panda and her friends at a party. Maybe . . .

"Look, I've done you a favor, keeping my mouth shut," Tyler sighed. "All I'm asking for is one back."

A great idea formulated in Mei's head. *Bingo!* "Hmm . . . I'll do it, but it'll cost you one—no, two—hundred bucks!"

Tyler seemed unfazed. "Okay."

Mei's tail shot out from excitement. But she still played it cool. "Hold, please."

Mei dashed around the bleachers and back to the top to huddle with her friends, who had heard it all.

But Miriam did not have a good feeling about the whole thing. "Are you serious? You can't trust him!"

"It's a trap," Abby said.

Priya's stomach quaked from nerves. "This sounds like a boy-girl party." She thought of what her parents would think. "Are we allowed to go to boy-girl parties?"

"Guys," Mei said, "two hundred bucks will put us over the top! We have to do this. We'll meet at Tyler's, I'll do my thang, and then we'll bounce! Easy-peasy." Mei couldn't believe her luck! This was perfect!

"But—" Miriam said.

Mei had already moved on. She peered down at Tyler below the risers. "Hey, dorkbag. We're in. But you only get the panda for an hour. And we're not bringing any presents."

Tyler smiled and reached out a hand. "Deal."

Mei was so happy that she didn't even mind touching Tyler's disgusting hand. They shook on it.

Chapter 11

The night of Tyler's party, Mei glanced at Tyler's invitation in her bedroom to make sure she had the right time and address just before she had to leave.

"I'm heading off to Mathletes!" Mei said as she passed the kitchen. "See ya later!"

Ming and Jin were setting down dishes full of food. Ming looked up eagerly. "Wait! What about your dinner!" They had worked so hard to get everything made in time before Mei had to leave for Mathletes. "I made all your favorites!"

Mei was tempted, but she caught herself. "Thanks, but . . . Miriam's dad is ordering pizza. Save me leftovers?" She turned to go.

Ming was disappointed, then got an idea. "What if I come with you?"

"Wuh?" Mei said.

"What're you doing, linear equations? Geometry? I have a double-jointed elbow. Look—I can make a perfect circle!" She demonstrated her unique talent.

Ugh. Mei backed away. "Wow! Yeah . . . but it'll be super boring. Wouldn't you rather hang with Dad?"

Jin perked up a little. There was a new show they could watch together. "Ming—"

Ming looked at Jin. Though she adored her husband, he didn't need her like her daughter did. A good mother did not abandon her child in need. She turned back to Mei. "Let's get my flash cards!"

"But—" Mei said.

Ming grabbed Mei's arm and rushed her out of the house. There would be no ifs, ands, or buts! Mei was going through one of the hardest times in her life. Ming couldn't stand another night without being there for her daughter.

As they passed through the courtyard, Mei sweated bullets, wondering how she would get rid of her mother. She had a party to go to.

But Ming seemed pumped for action. "I was a Mathletes champ in grade eight, you know."

"Uh-huh," Mei said, only half listening as she tried to think of a way to get her mother to stay. Maybe she should have started a small porridge fire in the kitchen, so her mother would've had to help her father put it out. Now it was too late!

"They called me the Uncommon Denominator!" her mother continued as they headed toward the temple gate.

"Cool," Mei said. "Oh!" She remembered something. "*Jade Palace* is on tonight. You can't miss that, right?"

But Ming didn't hear. If she could just be with her daughter for a little while, maybe she would start to feel better about how things were between them. "Now, who's the weak link?" Ming asked, thinking of Mei's Mathletes team. "Priya and Abby seem bright enough, but Miriam . . ."

"Traffic's a nightmare!" Mei said. "I can just take the streetcar. You stay and rest. . . ."

Ming still wasn't listening. For all she knew, Miriam could be the roadblock to Mei's academic progress. "I mean, she's a nice girl," Ming said, "but maybe she's slowing you down."

"Mom, you really don't have to come!"

"Don't be silly. We're already on the way."

Desperate, Mei jumped in front of her mom, stopping her in her tracks. "But I don't want you to!" she blurted.

Ming cocked her head. What had her daughter just said? Before Ming could respond, she heard a cacophony of voices outside the gate. Then the door handles on the gate rattled. A couple of sleeping temple cats yowled and scattered. Suddenly, the temple gates flew open! Ming and Mei were blinded by a flash of light.

A squad of glamorous older women burst into the courtyard. Ming gasped. It was Ming's Auntie Ping and Auntie Chen, and their daughters, Lily and Helen. All were dressed to the nines in designer tracksuits, carrying fancy handbags and wearing movie-star sunglasses. Each woman wore a piece of jade jewelry: a ring, a hair comb, a bracelet, earrings. They were all cut from the same cloth: tough, proud, put-together, elegant, *and* sporty.

The women spoke at once when they saw Ming and Mei.

"Finally," Auntie Chen said. "Look, it's Mei-Mei."

The ladies descended upon Mei, pinching and poking and squeezing her.

"Mei-Mei, dear," Auntie Ping said.

"Hey, cuz," Helen said to Ming. "We're here! Surprise!"

"Yoo-hoo, Ming," Lily said.

"Aunties," Mei said through the commotion, "what are you doing here?"

"The ritual, silly," Auntie Ping said.

"She's lost weight," Lily said.

"No, no, no," Auntie Chen said, "she's gained weight!"

Suddenly, another woman spoke. "Ladies!"

Everyone froze. Mei's relatives parted, making way for . . .

Grandma.

Grandma was every bit as regal and intimidating in person as over the phone. She, too, was wearing sunglasses at night. She stepped forward, the undisputed matriarch of the entire family.

Mei stared at her, wide-eyed. *The woman never seems to age,* Mei thought. She was practically bionic.

Ming tensed. "Mother."

Grandma's gazed locked on Mei.

"Hey, Grandma . . . ," Mei said meekly. She could see her own double reflection in her grandmother's mirrored sunglasses.

Grandma took Mei's chin in her hand and examined her granddaughter's face from all angles. "Poor dear. It must be so difficult keeping that unruly beast at bay." She whipped off her sunglasses. Grandma had a scar on her cheek. It was barely perceptible, but Mei could still see it.

"Your family is here now, Mei-Mei," Grandma said. "We will take care of everything."

They ushered Mei toward the house, and Mei stared longingly at the temple gates. There was no way she could leave now. Grandma had plans, and crossing Grandma could be suicidal.

In the Lee family living room, Mei's relatives chatted about preparations for the ritual as Mei sat on the couch next to her mother, surrounded by gifts brought by her aunties. Her grandmother was perched on the easy chair.

"What a surprise," Ming said, "that you all came so early."

Grandma raised an eyebrow. "You need all the help you can get, Ming."

"Eat," Auntie Ping said to Mei as she shoved a piece of food in her mouth. Then another and another.

"Mmm," Mei said, chewing.

Auntie Chen touched Mei's red hair. "Your hair's so thick and healthy, like a pelt."

"I brought you face cream," Lily said to Mei. "Never too early to start taking care of your skin!"

"Oh, it's too fancy," Ming said. "Thank your aunties, Mei-Mei."

"Thank you, aunties," Mei said, her mouth still full of food. But instead of eating, she'd rather be making her way to her paying gig. Her concert ticket was at stake.

"I thought we could practice the chant later," Lily said. "It's been a while. I brought these lozenges. Helps warm up the pipes. . . ."

Jin walked in from the kitchen, serving fruit and tea to their guests.

"So," Grandma said. "Mei-Mei, you've been managing to keep the panda in?"

"Yup!" Mei lied. "Totally!"

Lily gave Mei a skeptical look. *"Really?"*

Ming stared at her cousin. Was she implying something about Mei? "What's that?" Ming said sharply.

"Well . . . ," Lily said. "It's a little hard to believe that Mei-Mei could control such a beast. She's just a child."

"It's true," Auntie Ping said. "If Mei-Mei's panda is anything like Ming's . . ."

The ladies shuddered.

Ming drew close to Mei as if to protect her. "Mei-Mei's

better than any of us at controlling the panda. She passed every trigger test, even the kitten box."

Helen, Lily, and Auntie Chen looked impressed.

"Wow, the kitten box?" Grandma remarked. "It's so irresistible. . . ."

Ming smiled at Mei, tucking a loose strand of hair behind her daughter's ear. "She just thinks of my love for her," Ming explained, "and it gives her strength to stay calm. We may have our ups and downs, but nothing can break our bond." Her eyes shone with pride.

Mei forced a smile. "Exactly." *Could everyone just hurry up?* She was going to be late.

The aunties were touched by Ming's and Mei's words. "That's sweet," Auntie Ping said.

"Wish my daughter felt that way," Auntie Chen murmured.

"Anyway," Mei said with a yawn, her arms outstretched. "Thanks for all the gifts, but I think I'll go to bed early. Keepin' that animal locked down sure takes a lot of energy!"

"Get some rest," said Ming.

"Night, everyone!" Mei said.

Mei's family wished her good night as she got up from the couch. She collected her family's gifts. With her arms full, she calmly turned and took a few steps, as though she were not actually about to do something wildly wrong, then dashed to her room.

Grandma watched Mei's exit. There was something about the way her granddaughter was acting that didn't add up.

When Mei got to her bedroom, she shut the door. Finally, she was free! She set down the gifts and shoved stuffed animals under her bedcovers to make it look like she was sleeping. She climbed onto her bed to get to the window. *Hold up.* She'd almost forgotten her transit pass. She reached for it on the nightstand and knocked a framed photo of herself and her mother to the floor. She didn't have time to pick it up. Mei was already halfway out the window when someone knocked on her door.

Now what? Mei scrambled back in, shut the window, and composed herself.

Grandma swept into the room before Mei could even say "Come in."

"Mei-Mei," Grandma said. "Can I have a word with you?"

"Uh . . . sure," Mei said. *But make it fast.* "What's up?"

Grandma pulled a kerchief from her pocket, unfolded it, and held up a tuft of red fur. "I found this."

Mei stared at her own fur. She knew she shed a lot, but the clump in Grandma's hand was ridiculous.

Grandma stared at her coolly. "Strange for a girl who hasn't let her panda out . . ."

"Uh . . ." Mei grabbed her trash can and held it in her

grandmother's direction. "It's not mine—" She wondered if Grandma would believe they had recently fostered a giant Bernese Mountain Dog.

"Mei-Mei," Grandma said. "I know what you're doing."

Mei swallowed. *She does?*

Grandma studied the fur in her hand. "I know how hard it is to keep the beast in. It feels so good to let it out. So free. But each time you do, the stronger it gets." She dropped the fur into the trash can. "You'll be bound to it forever, and the ritual will fail."

Mei didn't like how that sounded. "Has that ever happened?"

"It cannot happen," Grandma said quickly.

So . . . what did Grandma mean? Mei wondered. Had it happened or not?

"You know, your mother and I were close once. But the red panda took that away." She touched her scar.

Mei was stunned. *Wait a second.* Had her own mother, as a panda, hurt Grandma? Mei would never dream of doing anything to her own mother. Plus, her mother would kill her if she tried.

"I couldn't bear to see that happen to you," Grandma said as returned to the door. "So no more panda." She paused. "You are your mother's whole world, Mei-Mei. I know you'll do what's right."

Grandma closed the door, leaving Mei in darkness.

Mei bit her lip. *This is not good.* She thought of her duties for Tyler's party and her grandmother's words.

To panda or not to panda?

That was the question.

Chapter 12

Party lights flashed in the windows of an ornate McMansion as music played. Tyler had the whole house to himself. He had managed to convince his parents that they should go out on a date, something they hadn't done in years. He swore up and down that he'd be the responsible man they'd raised him to be. He was thirteen, after all. Practically an adult. "It is time to trust," he had said. His parents had eaten it up. *Suckers.*

In Tyler's living room, about twenty-five boys occupied one end of it. Opposite the boys, roughly the same number of girls were gathered, as far away as possible. The vibe in the room would best be described as *lame*, the exact opposite of what Tyler had in mind.

Tyler was sitting on one of the couches, arms crossed. He looked at his watch again. It was 7:42. His star attraction was a no-show. He glared at Miriam, who was sitting on a sofa with Priya and Abby. "Where is she?" he said.

Miriam let out a weak laugh and tried to act like nothing was wrong. "Who's up for some Boggle?" No one replied.

Miriam and her friends did their best to stall. They started up a game of charades.

Priya did a strange interpretive dance in the middle of the room.

"Uh . . . ," Miriam said. "Worm!"

"Octopus!" Abby said.

"Spaghetti?" Miriam guessed.

"Killer robot!" Abby said.

A goth girl spoke up. "Mortality."

Priya stopped. "Nice."

"This sucks," said a boy, bored out of his mind.

"Let's bail," said a girl.

The other kids began to murmur, restless.

"Just wait!" Miriam said. "She'll be here."

Tyler glared at Miriam. "I knew she'd flake!"

Then the doorbell rang. Everyone brightened, full of hope.

"Panda Girl!" a boy said.

"It's Mei!" a girl said.

"That's her!" kids said.

"Thank Cthulhu!" Priya remarked.

Tyler ran to the door. "About time . . ." He threw the door open.

There was Mei, standing in Tyler's doorway, wearing the red panda cardboard costume she wore when she gave temple tours.

The party guests stared at her in confusion.

"Wha—?" said one.

"Huh?" said another.

"Yo!" Mei said, panting. "What up, peeps?"

Tyler stepped closer, angry. "What are you wearing?"

Mei chuckled and tried to pretend it was all part of the plan. "Heyyyy, Tyler . . . happy birthday. . . ."

"I'm paying for the red panda," Tyler fumed. "Not this garbage! Deal's off!"

"Wait!" Mei said, dancing wildly in her costume. "Can garbage do this?" She started gyrating. "C'mon, guys." She acted out another dance move. "Stir the porridge, stiiiirrrr the porridge—ah!"

Miriam, Priya, and Abby pulled Mei to the side, and they huddled together.

"Are you feeling okay?" Miriam said.

"Guys, it's hard to explain," Mei said. "But just . . . just trust me on this! I can't panda anymore. I'm sorry!"

Miriam could tell Mei was serious. Maybe Mei had gotten into trouble with her mother? "Okay, okay, okay," Miriam said. "It's fine. You don't have to do it. We'll just . . . uh . . . figure something—"

"I won't go," Priya said.

"What?" Mei said. "You can't not go! Jesse's your soul mate!"

Priya frowned. "But we only have enough for three tickets."

"Then I'll stay home," Abby said.

"Abby, no!" Mei said. "I'll stay home—"

"Guys," Miriam said, "if we can't all go, then none of us should go." They were besties. They stuck together. "Right?"

They sighed, knowing Miriam was right. They leaned on each other, at the verge of tears. Their dreams were slipping away. Miriam started sniffling. They would have to put off becoming women . . . for, like, an eternity.

Mei couldn't bear it. "Urgh! Just one last time." *What harm could sixty minutes of panda really cause anyway?*

She turned to face Tyler and his guests. "You want the panda? You're getting the panda!" Mei threw her hands up in the air, and—*phwaboom!* She *poof*ed into a panda in a cloud of pink smoke. "Let's hear it for the birthday boy!"

Miriam, Abby, and Priya looked at each other joyfully. Everyone, including Tyler's guests, cheered. Mei hoisted Tyler onto her shoulders as the party kicked into high gear.

Someone cranked up the stereo volume. Party music blasted from the speakers. Mei and her friends did everything they could to make Tyler feel like the star of the party. Tyler ate it up as everyone danced. Even the goth girl joined in. Soon Tyler was outside in his ginormous yard, riding on Panda Mei's back, whooping and hollering as she bounded across the lawn on all four paws.

"Faster!" Tyler ordered. "Faster! Woo!"

Miriam, Priya, and Abby hopped on, too.

"I'm king of the world!" Priya shouted.

The crowd cheered. Mei leaped into the air.

Back at Mei's house, Ming walked her family to the temple gates to see them off. It had been a long night. If she heard her mother correct her posture one more time, she'd lose it.

"You sure the hotel's all right?" Ming asked.

"It'll do," Auntie Ping replied. "At least breakfast is free."

"Get some rest," Auntie Chen said. "You look tired."

"G'night, cuz!" said Helen said. "Try that tea!"

"Good night, Ming," Lily said.

"Good night," said Ming.

Grandma was the last to exit. "Ming, this is a critical time," she said before she got into their limo. "Mei-Mei needs a strong hand now, more than ever. Don't let her out of your sight."

Ming nodded. She would add this request to the hundreds of others her mother had made all evening. "I won't, Mother," she said.

And with that, Grandma left. Ming closed the gate and took a moment for herself. She exhaled, then turned to the house, eager to check on Mei-Mei one last time before she went to bed. It was something she did almost every night.

Ming cracked the door to Mei's bedroom. She gazed at her daughter's sleeping form huddled under the covers. A breeze blew in. The window was open. Mei slipped into

Meilin Lee, or Mei for short, is a thirteen-year-old girl in Toronto.
With her energy and determination, she is a force of nature!

Mei is a straight-A student.
Math, French, geography, music—Mei excels at it all!

Miriam, Abby, and Priya are Mei's loyal friends. These inseparable besties will do just about anything for each other.

Mei and her friends are self-proclaimed 4*Townies— mega-fans of the boy band 4*Town.

Ming is Mei's devoted mother. She thinks keeping her daughter well-fed will give her the energy to be the best that she can be!

As keepers of their family temple, Mei and Ming honor their ancestor Sun Yee, who was a scholar, poet, and defender of red pandas.

Jin is Mei's father and the chef of the family.
He inspects every dumpling Mei makes.

Mei's life is turned upside down when she wakes up one morning,
looks in the bathroom mirror, and realizes she has turned into
a red panda!

Mei panics when she hears her mother approaching the bathroom.

After figuring out how to transform back into a girl, Mei goes to school wearing a hat to cover her new red hair.

In order to keep from turning into a red panda, Mei must remain calm. That's nearly impossible when her archnemesis, Tyler, teases her.

Mei poofs into a red panda in class after her mother visits her at school and embarrasses her!

Mei tries to hide in the school bathroom,
but comes face-to-face with a shocked classmate.

Still a giant red panda, Mei rushes to get home,
leaping over buildings and cars on her way.

When they see Panda Mei, Miriam, Priya, and Abby freak out!

Feeling angry, sad, and confused, Panda Mei bursts into tears.
Her besties promise her that they will always love her, panda or not!

the room and reached across the bed, but she stepped on something that made a crunching sound. "Oh!" Ming looked down to see the broken picture of her and Mei. "Oh, no!" She dropped to her knees and started picking up shards of broken glass. She was lucky she hadn't cut herself. She reached under the bed to pick up another piece of glass when she noticed something.

She pulled out a red panda T-shirt. "Huh?" She read the slogan. " 'Fur baby?' "

Ming grabbed the bedside lamp, turned it on, and dived under Mei's bed. "What!"

Mei's hideaway was full of panda merch, pics of herself as a panda, and fan letters. Then Ming saw crumpled assignments with abysmal grades. *That couldn't be Mei-Mei's work, could it?* And there was a huge stash of cash! *Where could my daughter get that kind of money?* Then she noticed Tyler's birthday flyer that highlighted Red Panda Girl's special appearance. "What in . . ."

Ming got to her feet. "Mei-Mei! What is all this—" She threw back the covers and revealed a pile of Mei's stuffed animals. Wilfred simply stared at her.

Chapter 13

Back at Tyler's party, Mei and her besties hung out on Tyler's roof. When everyone was distracted with cake, they had snuck off and found the best place to take a break, courtesy of Panda Mei's high jumping skills. They had a gorgeous view of Toronto's evening skyline.

Mei, still a panda, stuffed birthday cake into her mouth. "We did it!" she cheered. "We are seeing 4*Town! Wooo!"

"Yes!" Priya said.

"Woo-hoo!" Abby echoed.

They all made a toast with pieces of cake and listened to a radio they had borrowed from Tyler's house. It played music from a local Top 40 station.

"Hey!" they heard Tyler say from down below. "Anyone seen Mei?"

The girls ducked, then peered over the roof edge to check out the situation. Tyler was in the yard with some of his guests, scanning the area.

"Dang," Priya said. "He is working you!"

"Ugh," Abby added. "What a diva!"

Abby wound up her arm like she was going to throw her plate of cake at Tyler, but Miriam stopped her.

"It'll all be worth it," Mei said, satisfied. She lay back on the roof and relaxed. *Pwooof!* Mei turned back into a girl. They settled back and looked at the sky. The moon hung low, huge and bright.

"Tomorrow," Mei said, "we are walkin' into that concert as girls, and comin' out women."

Miriam held up her arm. "Literally goose bumps."

"Mmm," Priya said. "What do you think Jesse smells like?"

Miriam stared dreamily at the sky. "Milk chocolate and wet rocks."

"Oh, yes," Abby agreed.

"Wow," Mei said. She pulled out her digital pet game from her pocket. "It's happening, Robaire Junior!" she said. "You're finally gonna meet your daddy!"

"And your hot uncles," Abby said.

Miriam turned to Mei. "What if you didn't do the ritual? What if you kept the panda?"

"What!" Mei exclaimed.

"Look at you!" Miriam said. "You're not the same feather-dustin', straight-A, goody-goody—"

"—who we never saw," Priya cut in. "Like, ever."

"Yeah!" Abby agreed.

"You're such a rebel now," Miriam said.

"Guys," Mei said, "I can't be like this forever! My

whole family would freak—especially my mom." Mei felt her stomach drop. "All her hopes and dreams are pinned on me."

"I know," Miriam said, "but you've really changed, and . . . I'm proud of you. Just don't get rid of all of it, ya know?"

"Yeah," Abby said. "If it weren't for you, none of this would be happening. You the bomb!"

"Word," Priya said. "You da bomb, Mei."

"No," Mei said. "YOU da bomb!"

"WE ALL DA BOMB!" Miriam cheered.

"Yes, yes!" Mei said to the sky. "We da bomb!"

They howled and screamed at the moon and stars, and then they all put their hands in.

"Robaire," Mei said, "I love you! We're comin' for you!"

"Yas!" said Priya.

"We are awesome," Abby agreed.

"4*Town!" Miriam said. "Yes!"

They wiggled their fingers together and group-hugged. Friends for life!

As the girls hugged, the radio played on. "Aight, homies," the DJ said, "next up is 4*Town! The boys are coming to Toronto on the twenty-fifth! So get your tickets now. . . ."

The girls froze.

The twenty-fifth? Mei thought.

"And check it," the DJ continued. "They'll be crankin'

open the stadium dome and performin' under a red lunar eclipse! It's gonna be galactic for sure—"

"Abby," Mei said, "you said the concert is the eighteenth."

Abby pulled the concert flyer from her pocket. "It is! He's wrong—look! The eighteenth, Toronto!"

The girls gathered around Abby.

"Uh, this says Toledo," Priya pointed out.

Abby gaped. "What?" She started muttering in Korean. "What the heck is Toledo?"

"Oh, no . . . ," said Miriam. "4*Town's the same night as the ritual?"

Mei *phwoomp*ed into a panda. "Noooooo! The same night? The same night? What?" She started hyperventilating.

"Mei," Miriam said. "Chill!"

"It's okay," Priya said.

"No, it isn't!" Mei said. "I can't miss 4*Town! We worked so hard!" She held her head in her paws. "The ritual! I'll let everyone down! No, no, no—"

"Hey!" Tyler called up. "Panda girl!"

Mei groaned. They'd been discovered.

The girls peered over the roof edge. Tyler was on the ground, yelling up at them. His guests had gathered around, drawn by the commotion.

"What're you doing?" Tyler said. "We want more rides!"

"Buzz off, jerkface," Mei said. "I'm busy."

Some of the kids snickered.

"Oh, snap!" someone said.

"You gonna take that, Tyler?" said another.

There was no way Tyler was going to be the laughingstock at his own party. He'd show Mei who was boss. "You want your money?" he said. "Then get your butt down here NOW!"

Mei's fur stood on end. Who did Tyler think he was? *She* was the one dealing with a true crisis! "Forget your money and forget YOU!"

Some of the kids gasped. Mei's eyes felt like they were on fire. Her friends tried to pull her back from the edge of the roof.

"Mei," Miriam said, "let's just go!"

Mei snarled.

"What about our deal?" Tyler said.

"Shove your deal!" Mei said.

"Fine!" Tyler shouted. "Get outta here. Go back to your psycho mom and your creepy temple, you FREAK!"

More kids gasped.

Mei couldn't take it anymore. She let out a feral roar and dove off the roof.

Kids started screaming. Mei's friends tried to call her back.

"Mei!"

"No!"

Mei leaped on top of Tyler. "Take it back!" she shouted. "Don't talk about my family like that! *Agh!* I hate you, I HATE—"

"Help!" Tyler cried. "Get offa me! I'm sorry! Don't hurt me! I'm sorry!"

But it was too late. She pulled back her furry arm and swiped his face with her paw.

"Mei-Mei!" It was Ming. "Stop! What is going on here?"

Mei looked up to see her mother standing over her, out of breath, clutching her car keys. Her eyes were wide with shock.

Suddenly, Mei realized what she had just done to Tyler. His cheek was bleeding. *Oh, no.*

Tyler was a terrified wreck. "I'm sorry," he sobbed. "Get offa me . . . please."

Mei looked around. Every single kid at the party was staring at her. In fear.

Chapter 14

Before long, Tyler's parents were standing outside in the driveway with Tyler and his party guests. Tyler's parents were saying angry words to Ming. Mei, who had turned back into a girl, was standing several yards away, with Miriam, Abby, and Priya by her side.

Tyler's mom shouted at Ming as she put a protective arm around her son. "I can't believe you would let your daughter do this!"

Tyler's dad looked like he was seconds from calling the police. "Do you understand what she did to my boy?"

"We live in a civilized society!" Tyler's mom added.

"I'm so sorry." Ming lowered her head, deeply apologetic.

Mei watched, ashamed.

"She's never done anything like this before," Ming pleaded with them in a soft, conciliatory tone. "I don't know what came over her. I'm sorry. . . ."

Tyler's father glared at Ming. "I don't want to hear your apologies, okay?"

Tyler's parents strode past Mei as though she were invisible.

"She's an animal," Tyler's mom said.

"All right, party's over," Tyler's father said. "Everyone go home!"

Tyler's parents took Tyler inside.

As the party guests scattered, Ming walked over to Mei. Mei braced herself, her heart sinking . . . but Ming walked right past her.

Her gaze was focused on Miriam, Priya, and Abby. "I can't believe you girls would use her like this!"

"What?" Miriam said, surprised that anyone would think that.

"But we didn't—" Priya said.

"Yeah, we'd never!" said Abby.

Mei couldn't believe what her mother was accusing them of. "Wha—?"

"I knew you were trouble," Ming said, ignoring their replies. "Putting all these thoughts in Mei-Mei's head! Parading her around! Now she's lying, sneaking out—she ATTACKED a defenseless boy! You think this is a joke? Do you know how dangerous this is?"

Miriam tried to speak up. "We didn't mean to— W-we just wanted to see 4*Town—"

"4*Town?" Ming cut in. "You manipulated her for a bunch of tacky delinquents?"

"No," Miriam said. "She wanted to—"

"Don't you blame her!" Ming said. "She is a good girl, and you've taken advantage of her!"

"Mei!" Miriam said. "Tell her."

The three friends stared at Mei, waiting for her to save them.

Mei looked at her mom. She couldn't bear to disappoint her any more than she already had. She'd hit a boy, even drawn blood. Tyler didn't need stitches, but her loving mom was not a person you should maul someone in front of—not after all her mother had done for Mei, to give her a future. What kind of ingrate daughter was she? No—correction. What kind of *delinquent* was Mei turning into? Her mom's worst nightmare? No, she couldn't—she couldn't be *that* to her mother.

Mei turned away from her friends.

"What?" Priya said in disbelief.

"Dude!" Abby said.

Miriam could hardly look at Mei.

"Come on, Mei-Mei," Ming said, vindicated. "Let's go." She held out her hand, and Mei took it.

In the car, Mei stared ahead from the passenger seat, silent as Ming started the engine. Ming backed out of the driveway and turned onto the street. Miriam, Priya, and Abby receded into the distance. Mei couldn't believe she had done that to her friends. Mei glanced at Ming, whose gaze was focused on the road. Her expression was unreadable. Then Ming reached out and placed a hand over Mei's. At least her mother still believed in her. But that had come at a cost.

Miriam, still standing in Tyler's driveway, had watched the car drive off. Then she noticed something on the ground where Mei had been standing. It was Robaire Junior, Mei's digital pet.

A week passed. Fans milled around the stadium where the 4*Town concert was being held, camped out to get the best seats. Posters of the 4*Town boys surrounded the venue, and a giant electronic billboard read 4*TOWN TONIGHT.

Miriam, Priya, and Abby went up to the box-office window. They had decided that they would go to the concert without Mei after all. Besties stuck together, and Mei could hardly be described as part of their group now.

A chipper clerk took their order. "All righty, general admission, eh? How many tickets?"

The girls looked at each other and sighed. They still missed Mei. It was like they were all grieving. Miriam shoved their portion of the cash through the ticket window. "Three, please."

In the temple courtyard, Mei sat with Mr. Gao and her family around a table for dinner. The evening was beautiful.

She looked up to see a giant number four flickering in the sky. Mei sighed. She knew it had to be a projection from the concert.

Mei wasn't the only one who had noticed. Grandma pointed at the number in horror. "What is THAT?"

Her relatives stopped chatting to look up.

"Um . . . I think it's coming from the stadium, Mother," said Ming.

Grandma shook her head. "Four is the worst number."

"You know," Lily said. "Vivian was due on the fourth, but I held her in until the fifth—"

"Quiet, Lily," Grandma interrupted. "Hurry up, everyone! It's almost time to start the ritual."

Mr. Gao noticed Mei didn't look so great. "Nervous, Mei-Mei?"

"A little," Mei said.

"I've got fifty years' experience as a shaman," said Mr. Gao. "This will be a piece of cake."

"Thanks, Mr. Gao," said Mei.

"And mostly painless," he added.

"Wait," Mei said, concerned. "Mostly?"

Grandma clinked her chopsticks against her glass.

Everyone immediately stopped talking.

Grandma cleared her throat. "Long ago, the spirits blessed the women of our family with a great challenge. Mei-Mei, tonight is your turn."

Mei's stomach quaked. She didn't like it when her aunties and her mother stared at her like that. Talk about performance anxiety!

"Like all the women around this table," Grandma continued, "you will banish the beast within and finally become your true self. May Sun Yee guide you and keep you safe."

"Hear, hear!" said Auntie Ping.

"That's right," Auntie Chen agreed.

"Mmm-hmm," added Helen.

"Don't blow it," Lily said.

Mei's stomach quivered again.

Ming gave Mei an encouraging smile.

Mr. Gao gazed at the full moon above. "It's almost time. The red moon is about to begin."

The women started clearing the table. Ming turned to Mei. "Mei-Mei, go get ready."

"Yes, Mother." Mei rose from the table and passed her father, who had been in the kitchen, cleaning up. He smiled at her. Mei wondered why she couldn't have taken after her father's side of the family. She smiled back.

As she continued to her room, her smile evaporated. Jin noticed.

"Jin!" Grandma called. "Help!"

Jin hurried to obey Grandma's order. He picked up some folding chairs from the courtyard and returned them to the basement. When he placed them in a corner, he bumped a table and his video camera fell to the floor. The viewfinder popped open and a video began to play.

The sound of Mei laughing with her friends came from the camera.

Jin picked it up and adjusted his glasses to get a better look. "Huh," he said as he watched Mei beatboxing and singing with her friends.

Jin looked up at the ceiling in the direction of Mei's room. Mei must have forgotten to delete her video after she'd used his camera.

In her bedroom, Mei stood in front of her full-length mirror. She was wearing a white ceremonial robe. She pinned a flower clip to her hair. Suddenly, Tyler's terrified face flashed through her mind. She heard herself screaming, "I HATE YOU!"

Mei gasped. Her heart raced. She let out a long breath to calm down and put on a tight smile. She needed to stay calm and focused on the ritual.

Someone knocked on her door.

"Come in," Mei said.

It was Jin.

"Hey, Dad," Mei said as he walked in. "I'm almost ready."

Jin held out the video camera. "Did you make this?"

Mei's smile faded as she reached for the camera. In the

viewfinder, she was a panda in all her glory, hugging her friends. "Here, I'll erase it."

Jin pulled the camera away.

"What? We were just being stupid," Mei explained. "The panda's dangerous. Outta control."

"You sound like your mother," Jin said. "What has she told you about her panda?"

"Nothing." Mei sighed. "She won't talk about it."

"It was quite destructive," Jin recalled. "She almost took out half the temple."

Mei's eyes widened. "You . . . you saw it?"

"Only once. She and your grandma had a terrible fight."

"Over what?" Mei asked.

Jin pointed to himself.

Meilin was stunned.

"Your grandma didn't approve of me," Jin explained. "But you should've seen your mom. She was . . . incredible."

Mei's cheeks burned. She only wished she was as incredible as her mother. "But . . . I'm a monster."

Jin looked at the video as it played. "People have all kinds of sides to them, Mei. And some sides are . . . messy. The point isn't to push the bad stuff away. It's to make room for it, live with it."

He passed the videocam to his daughter. "Mei, erase it if you want. But this side of you"—he paused to chuckle—"made me laugh."

Mei looked at the video. In it, Panda Mei was flanked by her laughing besties. She poured snacks into her own gullet and then hugged her friends close.

"Mei-Mei!" Ming called.

Mei hid the video camera as Ming opened the door. She looked anxious.

"It's time," said Ming.

Chapter 15

Mei followed her parents to the temple courtyard, which had been transformed for the ritual. The air was heavy with incense. Lanterns and hundreds of candles illuminated the evening. Grandma, her aunties, and Mr. Gao all waited for Mei to join them. Mei felt a pang of fear course through her body.

Mr. Gao stepped forward. "Just follow my directions," he said, "and breathe."

He led her down the steps to the center of the gathering. Mei kneeled as Mr. Gao drew a wide chalk circle around her. Mei took in a breath. This was it.

"Now don't move from the circle, you understand?" he said, his voice low. "For as long as the red moon shines, the astral realm will be open. And this circle is the door."

Mr. Gao signaled to Auntie Chen, who struck an ancient chime bowl. The other aunties, each with their own traditional Chinese instrument, joined in the rhythm. They began to chant in Cantonese.

"What are they saying?" Mei asked.

"The door will open only if we sing from our hearts. It doesn't matter what. I like Tony Bennett, but your grandma . . . she's from old school. Now, focus on their voices . . . let them guide you."

Mei did as she was told and closed her eyes. Soon, the circle began to glow.

Mr. Gao carried a sword in one hand, and raised his other arm to the sky. "Oh, Sun Yee," he intoned, "revered ancestor, hear us now!"

In the sky, the red lunar eclipse began. The moon started to turn a faint red.

"Guide this girl through her inner storm," Mr. Gao said.

The crimson moon grew stronger, bathing everything in a red light. The wind swirled around them. The lanterns swung. Mei opened her eyes briefly as her body began to slowly rise from the floor and float.

"Louder," Mr. Gao ordered. "Louder!"

Everyone did as they were told.

"Return the red spirit from where it came!" Mr. Gao shouted.

He held up his sword. A focused beam of red moonlight refracted off a gem on the hilt and landed on Mei. Her body was wreathed in wisps of energy. Then the circle flashed with blinding light.

Mei opened her eyes. She found herself standing in a lush bamboo forest. A red moon hovered above. A sudden wind sent a trail of leaves flying before her. Then the wind gently gave Mei a push.

The forest was quiet. She walked among the trees and followed the trail of leaves swirling in the air. She stumbled into a clearing. Those leaves were met by other leaves that rose from the ground and entwined. Mei shielded her eyes as a bright light appeared above her. Then the light descended, revealing . . .

"Sun Yee," Mei whispered.

She bowed before the stunning woman dressed in imperial robes. Sun Yee's long hair flowed behind her, carried by the wind.

Sun Yee returned the bow, then formed a wide circle with a ribbon. The circle became a mystical mirror.

Mei stared at her reflection. She looked just like her human self, but she had dark hair again. Mei raised her hand to touch the mirror. It moved at her touch, like water. As her hand passed through the mirror, a ghostly red panda paw reached toward her from the other side.

Mei gasped. She pulled her hand back and looked up at Sun Yee for guidance, but her ancestor's expression was neutral.

Mei reached out both arms and stepped toward the mirror. As she moved through the mirror, her image began to split in two. The mirror separated her selves, like a prism. On the left was Panda Mei. On the right was human Mei with dark hair. Mei gritted her teeth and pushed further. She could do this. She *had* to do this.

In the courtyard, Mei's family and Mr. Gao continued to chant in Cantonese. In the center of the glowing circle, Mei's body was still levitated. Her body began to writhe from the struggle.

Ming and Jin exchanged looks of concern as they chanted. Ming wondered if Mei would be strong enough to get through the ritual.

In the astral plane, Mei continued to push her way through the mirror. She cried out. Now the pain was nothing like she had ever experienced before. It emanated from deep within, like thunder rolling through her body. Her red panda howled. The mirror was dividing them, but they were so tightly bound, the separation was absolute agony.

In the courtyard, Mr. Gao held up a talisman that looked just like Ming's. The panda spirit roared as it came out of Mei and was pulled into the talisman.

"Mei-Mei!" Ming cried. "You can do it. Keep going!"

But Mei couldn't hear her mother. She could only hear the deafening roars from her panda, who was now behind her as she pushed through. One more step and Mei would be completely out of the mirror. She gave one final look back at her red panda on the opposite side of the mirror. Her panda looked like it was frightened, and in pain. They locked gazes. Images from all the incredible moments she had experienced as Panda Mei flashed through her mind. She realized that her panda was sometimes angry and out of control, but it was also joyful, excited, kind, and full of wonder. Mei's eyes widened. She remembered her father's words. THIS was who she really was—the highs, the lows, the good, and the bad. The panda was HER. She couldn't give herself up so easily.

"Nooooooo!" Mei cried. She immediately stopped and reversed direction. She ran toward her panda.

Phwaboom! The temple ground shook and filled with red smoke. Everyone around the circle was thrown back. Through the smoke, a large form emerged.

It was Panda Mei, in all her glory.

Chapter 16

Mei looked at herself, ecstatic. She was a panda again! Her entire family was still disoriented from the smoke.

"What was that?" asked Helen.

The smoke began to clear, and Grandma gasped at Panda Mei. Mei's aunties were stunned, while Ming looked at her daughter in horror.

"Mei-Mei!" cried Ming, reaching out to her. "It's okay! We can do it again."

Mei recoiled.

"Mei-Mei?" Ming said.

"I'm keeping it," Mei said.

Grandma couldn't believe her ears. "What did she say?"

Everyone murmured their shock and disappointment.

"I'm keeping it!" Mei repeated. She turned and ran.

"Mei-Mei!" Ming shouted.

"Stop her!" Grandma commanded.

Everyone rushed forward and grabbed Mei.

Ming pleaded with her daughter. "What are you doing? No, Mei-Mei!"

"Let go!" Mei begged, struggling against her family.

"What's come over you?" Ming exclaimed.

Mei continued to resist as everyone tried to keep her within the temple gates.

"Mei-Mei!" Grandma shouted. "Listen to your mother!"

"NO!" Mei dug in further. Finally, she jerked away with all her might, and everyone fell backward.

The talisman that hung from Ming's neck hit the ground and cracked!

"I'm going to the concert!" Mei yelled, and then sprinted through the temple gates.

"Get back here!" Ming yelled.

Mei kept going.

Ming clenched her fists and heaved with fury.

"This is a disaster," said Grandma. "Unbelievable! How could she do this? Ming! How could you let this happen? She's out of control! Ming! Answer me! What are we going to do about Mei-Mei! Her life is ruined . . . forever!"

Ming could feel the blood rushing in her ears. Her cracked talisman began to glow red. Is this what her own life amounted to? Toiling day after day to raise a child who could throw it all away in a split second for a bunch of . . . of . . . singing *derelicts*?

Jin rushed to Ming's side. "Ming, it's okay."

Ming's talisman splintered.

She rose to her feet. "How could she . . . how could she do this to her own mother?"

Wind whipped through the courtyard. The family looked on in shock as bright light shot out of Ming's talisman. A vaporous red form emerged. It was Ming's red panda spirit—enormous and enraged! The gargantuan spirit leaped to the top of the temple gates, looked down at Ming with glowing white eyes, and then hurtled toward her. Ming fell to the ground, unconscious. Then her body levitated and began to glow.

"Ming?" said Jin.

Grandma shouted *"Oh, no!"* in Cantonese.

Ming snapped back to consciousness and screamed with rage. "MEI-MEI!"

Meanwhile, Panda Mei sprinted down the middle of the street in the direction of the 4*Town concert.

Random pedestrians saw the giant panda and scattered. Mei hardly noticed. " 'Scuse me!"

A car horn honked, startling Mei. She *poof*ed into a girl, and the very process propelled her high into the air and out of the path of speeding traffic. *That was weird, but COOL!* Mei thought. Exhilarated, she realized she could use her *poof*ing power like a turbo booster. She tried *poof*ing again and landed on a nearby rooftop. Pigeons scattered. She laughed and *poof*ed again into a panda. She flew through the air and spotted the swirling stadium spotlights ahead.

She surged forward, cleared the opening of the dome, and dropped toward the crowd below. She saw her besties and sailed toward them. Just before she hit the ground, Mei *poof*ed back into a girl and landed safely alongside Miriam, Priya, and Abby.

Her friends coughed from all the smoke.

"Mei?" Miriam and Priya said.

"MEI?" Abby said. "You're here!"

"What are you doing here?" Miriam said.

Mei looked at her friends, out of breath. "I couldn't do it. The panda's a part of me. And you guys are, too."

"Mei, you threw us under the bus." Miriam turned her back on Mei.

"I know, and I'm sorry," Mei said. "I've been, like, obsessed with my mom's approval my whole life. I couldn't take losing it." She teared up. "But losing you guys feels even worse!"

"Well, too bad," Miriam said. "'Cause you did." But as the words left her mouth, Miriam found herself wishing they could all be a crew again.

Mei's heart broke.

Suddenly, Mei heard a barely perceptible high-pitched sound among all the crowd noise. *Beep! Beep!*

Mei's eyes widened. Was that . . . "Robaire Junior?"

Priya smiled. "Miriam's been taking care of him twenty-four-seven!"

"And singing him lullabies every night," Abby said.

Miriam covered their mouths with her hands. "No, I haven't! They're lying," she said to Mei.

Beep! Beep!

Miriam groaned as she pulled the digital pet from her pocket. "Here. Found him at Tyler's."

Mei looked at Robaire Junior, and then at Miriam. "4*Town forever?"

Miriam couldn't resist. She gave in. "4*Town forever."

Mei and Miriam embraced. Abby and Priya piled in and turned it into a group hug. "4*Town forever," they said.

As they hugged, Miriam spotted a familiar boy in the crowd. "Tyler?"

The girls broke from their hug.

Tyler was standing nearby, covered head to toe in 4*Town merchandise. He gasped. "Tyler?" he said in a deep voice. "Who's Tyler? I don't know a—"

"You . . . are . . . a 4*Townie?" Mei asked.

Tyler froze.

The girls squealed and wrapped him in a hug.

"No way!" Miriam said.

"O.M.G. Welcome to the sisterhood," Priya said.

"YEAH!" yelled Abby.

"He's one of us!" Mei said.

"Whatever, dorks," said Tyler.

Finally, the girls let go. Miriam turned to Mei. "Your mom must've gone nuclear."

"Who cares?" Mei said. "What's she gonna do, ground me?"

The girls cracked up.

At that moment, the stadium lights dramatically dimmed. The crowd roared. The concert was starting! The crowd chanted, "4*Town! 4*Town! 4*Town!"

"This is it! Miriam said, grabbing Tyler by the shoulders and shaking him.

"Is this real life?" Priya said.

"Guys!" Mei said, swooning. "Hold me!"

Mei's friends surrounded her and held on tight while they freaked out.

A big screen lit up and a countdown began.

"Four!" the crowd shouted, "three . . . two . . . one!"

Dramatic lights revealed five cages slowly rising from the stage floor.

"Yes!" Mei shrieked.

One by one, the 4*Town members burst from their cages and greeted their fans. First Aaron T. emerged.

"Oh my GOSH!" screamed Miriam.

Next was Aaron Z.

Tyler shouted, "Yeah! Z! I love you, man!"

Tae Young was up next.

Abby professed her love in Korean.

Then Jesse stepped out, blowing a kiss toward the crowd. Priya melted. "Yes! Jesse!"

There was only one cage left. . . .

It broke open, and Robaire stepped out. "Toronto!" he called. "Who knows what's up?"

Mei and her friends clung to each other—their eyes bugging out, faces sweating, hearts thumping wildly. "You know what's up!" they screamed in unison.

Little did Mei and her friends know that in the distance, a huge dark form towered over Toronto's buildings. As it moved forward, the ground shook.

Thwoom.

Thwoom.

Thwoom.

Chapter 17

Mei and her friends joined the crowd in another round of uproarious cheering as a song began.

"Gimme one! Two! Three! Four!" Robaire and his fellow boy-band members unfurled wings and ascended, suspended from wires attached to the scaffolding above the stage. They looked like angels floating in the air.

This is *heaven,* Mei thought. The crowd went wild.

Robaire reached out a hand as he sang. To Mei, it looked like was singing to her. Mei and her friends pushed through the crowd toward the stage, screaming. Mei had to get to Robaire. Through some miracle, they managed to make it to the edge of the stage. Mei's friends lifted her up, and Mei stretched out her hand toward Robaire.

His eyes locked with hers, his hand still outstretched.

Mei could hardly breathe. Just as their fingertips were about to touch . . .

"MEI-MEI!" roared a giant-panda-Ming-like voice.

Mei looked up, totally bewildered. A terrifying red panda face appeared in the opening of the dome roof!

Mei's friends and everyone else in the stadium screamed, including 4*Town.

"Mom?" Mei shouted.

Ming roared, then dropped onto the stage with an enormous thud. The impact sent the 4*Town boys swinging on their wires. When the dust settled, it became clear just how big Ming was. She pulled herself to her full height. She was as tall as the stadium itself. And she let out a deafening roar.

The crowd shrieked and began to scatter. Mei was blind with terror. *That* could not be her mom. She turned and ran for an exit. Her friends followed close behind.

Ming roared again, shaking the stadium.

Suddenly, Mei heard her father's voice. "Mei!"

She turned and spotted her dad, Mr. Gao, Grandma, and her aunties through the running masses of people. They raced up to her.

"Dad?" Mei said.

"We have to save your mother!" Grandma exclaimed.

"She's gone loco!" Auntie Chen said.

"Mei," Jin said. "We have to do the ritual again."

"We gotta turn her back," said Helen.

A giant shadow passed over them. Mei turned and saw a huge paw descending toward her—

"Mei-Mei!" Ming roared.

Mei screamed and tried to make a break for it, but she was too late. The paw grabbed her.

"No!" Mei shouted as was hoisted into the air.

"Ming! She's your daughter!" cried Lily.

"Mei!" Jin cried.

Mei struggled in Ming's grip.

Ming glared at her. "You are in big trouble, young lady!"

Miriam, Priya, Abby, and Tyler waved their arms and screamed at the top of their lungs.

"Mrs. Lee! No! Stop!" yelled Miriam.

"Leave her alone!" Priya said.

"Don't hurt her!" Abby said.

"Let her go!" Tyler exclaimed. "You . . . Momzilla! You . . . psycho bathmat!"

Mei struggled to break free, but Panda Ming's grip was too strong.

Ming turned toward the stage. Her voice was full of rage. "I'm shutting this down right now!" Ming grabbed the giant 4*Town sign from the set and tore it away. The impact sent the trapped 4*Town boys swinging from their wires again.

"NO! MOM!" cried Mei.

Ming turned and yelled at the fleeing crowd. "Everyone, go home!" she said. "Where are your parents? Put some clothes on!"

She threw the 4*Town sign on the ground, and then looked down at Mei in her grip. "This isn't you."

Mei stared up at her mother. The concert was destroyed. Her dreams had been destroyed. And the destroyer was her own mother.

Mei's eyes took on a red glow. "This . . . is ME!"

Phawwwwooomph!

Mei exploded into her panda form. Then she opened her mouth wide and bit her mother's paw. *Hard.*

Ming roared in pain, releasing her grip on Mei. The family watched as Mei plummeted through the air. Grandma and Jin gasped.

Moments before impact, Mei *poof*ed back into a girl, which softened her landing. Her friends and family rushed to her.

"Mei!" said Jin. "Are you okay?"

Her aunties and friends all talked at once.

"Ay-yah!"

"Mei-Mei!"

"Are you hurt?"

Mei barely registered her fall from the sky. She *poof*ed back into a panda and let Ming have it. "I'm not your little Mei-Mei anymore! I LIED, MOM!" she shouted.

"What? Ming said, shocked.

"It was my idea to hustle the panda!" Mei shouted. "My idea to go to Tyler's party! It was all me! I like boys! I like loud music! I like gyrating! I'm thirteen! DEAL WITH IT!"

Mei's family and friends were shocked.

Ming paused for a moment, then threw her head back and let out a thunderous roar.

"The ritual!" exclaimed Grandma. "Everyone, in position! Mei-Mei! Keep her busy!"

"Oh, I'll keep her busy," Mei said, just before she rushed toward her mother, growling.

"Where's Jin?" Grandma said. "Jin!"

Jin was already sprinting around the stadium with a baseball line marker, drawing a circle large enough for his giant panda wife. "Mei! Keep her in the circle!" he yelled.

Mr. Gao looked up. The red moon eclipse was waning. With a look of determination, he climbed the steps to the top of the stadium. Given Ming's enormous size, he needed to get to a higher point to conduct the ritual.

Ming tried to grab Mei as Mei played a game of keep-away with her mother.

"Get back here!" Ming said, swiping at her. "You think you're so mature? Lying to me? Biting me? How could you be so, so crass?"

"Oh, that's nothing," Mei retorted. "You wanna see crass?"

Mei turned around, stuck out her rear, and started . . . *twerking.*

"Stop! No!" Ming roared. The vision of her gyrating daughter was burning her eyes. "What are you doing? Who taught you that? Put that away! Stop it!"

"Is this bothering you?" said Mei.

All her friends whooped and hollered as Mei danced.

Jin rushed past as he finished the circle. He shouted at Grandma and the aunties. "Start chanting. Now!"

"Ladies!" Grandma stepped up to the line and began the chant. The aunties hurried to join in.

Mei continued her wild dancing to distract her mother.

Grandma stared at the circle. It barely flickered. "Sing louder!"

"We're trying!" Auntie Chen said.

Miriam anxiously watched with Priya and Abby, then she heard something. She turned and saw 4*Town in the distance, untangling themselves from their harnesses.

"C'mon," Robaire said. "Let's get outta here!"

Miriam's face lit up. "C'mon!" she said to her friends. They all ran toward the 4*Town members.

Mei saw the flickering circle and redoubled her efforts to buy her family some time. She shook her furry tush faster. "Take it, Mom! TAKE IT!"

"Stop it!" Ming roared. "*Stooooooop!*" Ming whirled around and covered her eyes. Her tail swept through the air and smacked right into Mei. Grandma and the aunties ducked just in time.

Mei grabbed onto Panda Ming's tail and began climbing it. "All I wanted . . . was to go . . . to a concert!" she screamed.

Ming turned in a circle, trying to grab Mei. But Mei kept *poof*ing from girl to panda and back again, launching herself higher each time, which helped her evade her mother's monstrous paws.

"I never went to concerts," Ming said. "I put my family first. I tried to be a good daughter!"

Those words stung Mei. She *poof*ed back into a panda and leaped onto her mother's furry face. "Well, SORRY I'm not PERFECT!" she yelled, digging her claws into Ming's fur.

She *poof*ed back into a girl, rising in the air, crying hot, angry tears.

"Sorry I'm not good enough! And sorry I'll never be . . . LIKE YOU!"

Pwhooooph! She turned back into a panda and turbo-blasted toward her mother.

Mei head-butted Ming right between the eyes.

Ming roared in pain from the impact.

Mei ricocheted off her mother's head and hurtled through the air. She hit the ground hard and tumbled to a stop. *Poof!* She was a girl again. She lifted her head, dazed.

Her mother staggered backward and crashed to the ground, shaking the entire stadium.

Mei gasped. Her mother lay flat on her back, out cold. "Oh, no!" said Mei. Then she noticed the circle. Her mother's body was almost entirely outside it.

The circle dimmed, then flickered out.

"Mom, MOM!" Mei screamed. She looked up at the sky and saw that the red moon was ending.

Chapter 18

As the dust cleared, Jin, Grandma, and the aunties saw the aftermath of Mei and Ming's fight. They were stunned.

Mei *poof*ed into a panda and ran toward her mother. "Mom! You have to get in the circle!" She tried to pull Ming, but she wouldn't budge.

"Wake up," Mei cried. "I'm sorry, Mom. . . ." She had gone too far. Her mother was right. This wasn't who she was. She wasn't someone who would hurt her own mom. "Come on . . . please!"

Ming's chest heaved, but she didn't respond.

Mei strained with all her might. "Please!"

Grandma knew what she had to do. The job was just too big for one panda. Her daughter needed her. Her granddaughter needed her. She took a deep breath. "Sun Yee," she said, "give me strength." She raised an arm into the air, ripped off her bracelet, and smashed it to the ground.

Phwabooooooom! When the smoke cleared, elegant Grandma Panda was standing there.

Mei tugged at her mother, crying. She couldn't give up.

Suddenly, she felt something beside her. She turned to look. It was another red panda.

"Pull, Mei-Mei!" Grandma ordered.

"Grandma?" Mei said.

"I'm not losing my daughter!" Grandma yelled at Mei's aunties. "Don't just stand there!"

The women all looked at each other, then ran forward, grabbing their jade talismans and smashing them on the ground.

Poof! Poof! Poof! Poof! They all became pandas.

Mei was amazed.

"Make room for your elders, Mei-Mei," Auntie Panda Chen said as she pulled Ming's tail.

"We're with you," Auntie Panda Ping said.

"What are you doing?" Mei asked. "What if you can't turn back?"

"Your mom needs us," Panda Helen replied.

"She's family," Panda Lily said.

"Less talking, more pulling!" said Grandma.

"This fur is so itchy," said Panda Lily.

"Quiet, Lily!" snapped Grandma.

Ming's unconscious body began to slide, foot by foot, toward the circle. Grandma and the aunties began to chant.

Meanwhile, Mr. Gao had reached the top of the stadium. He looked down, barely able to hear everyone below. "Sing from the heart!" he shouted.

Jin heard Mr. Gao from above. The circle flickered, but

it wasn't enough. "Louder!" Jin yelled. "The circle isn't working!"

Then Mei heard the familiar sound of beatboxing. As she pulled on her mother, she turned to look at her friends, who were standing just outside the circle. Tyler tapped out a rhythm with a discarded set of drumsticks while Miriam, Abby, and Priya beatboxed in time.

The sight of her friends reenergized Mei. She pulled harder. Then a sweet, sweet voice rang out.

It was Robaire, singing her all-time favorite song. The other 4*Town boys joined in, singing in glorious, five-part harmony.

Mei's family chanted even louder as they pulled. Ming was almost fully in the circle now. Everyone's voices became a glorious fusion of beatboxing, singing, and chanting. Even die-hard fans who hadn't left the stadium emerged from their hiding places and came forward to help.

The circle burst into a bright glow!

Mei and her family kept singing. There was only a sliver of red moon left! Mr. Gao raised his sword and directed a beam of red moonlight down toward Ming.

The family tugged on Ming one last time just as the beam struck Ming's forehead. The circle glowed brighter than ever before. A strong wind blew through the arena. Ming, Mei, and her whole family of pandas floated upward. Mei saw a blinding flash! She squeezed her eyes shut.

When she opened her eyes, she had transformed into a girl again and was in the bamboo forest, alone.

Mei looked up at the sky. The red moon was faint. "Mom?" She got to her feet. "Mom!" Where was she? She pushed through the thick bamboo. Then she heard faint crying. She turned at the sound and broke into a run.

She pushed through the bamboo and spotted her mother in a clearing, sitting on the ground, hunched over. Her face was buried in her hands as she cried. Her mother's hair was red. It hung loose and spilled over her shoulders.

Mei approached her mother hesitantly. "Mom," Mei said. "Are you okay? We have to—

Ming looked up, revealing her face.

Mei stopped, startled by what she saw.

Her mother looked like she was sixteen! She was wearing glasses.

"Mom?" Mei said.

"I'm sorry," Ming said. "It's all my fault. . . ." She continued to sob.

Mei was stunned by the sight of her mother in such a vulnerable state. Ming had always been flawless to her, *perfect*.

Mei kneeled beside her mother. "What happened?"

"I—I hurt her," Ming said.

"Who?"

"My mom," Ming replied. "I got so angry . . . and I lost

control." Ming remembered the blowout fight they'd had. "I'm so sick of being perfect. I'm never going to be good enough for her. Or anyone."

Mei processed her mother's words. She realized that she and Ming were more similar than she ever knew. She smoothed her mother's hair. "I know it feels that way, like, all the time. But it isn't true." She stood and offered a hand. "C'mon."

Ming took her hand and rose to her feet. Mei led her through the forest. As they walked, Ming changed from a teenager to a young woman, then older. . . .

When Mei looked back, she saw the mom she knew. Mei faced forward, determined. Up ahead, she heard voices.

"Get ahold of yourselves. We have to find them!" Grandma said.

Mei led Ming into the clearing. Mei's aunties immediately started talking over each other when they saw Ming and Mei.

"You're okay! Hurry!" Auntie Ping said.

"There you are!" said Helen.

"Where you have you been? C'mon! Let's go!" said Lily.

Grandma interrupted them. *"Ladies."*

Mei's aunties hushed and made way for Grandma to step through.

Grandma went straight up to Ming and Mei with a stern look on her face. Ming looked down. Suddenly, Grandma hugged Ming. Ming let out a small gasp and stiffened. Then she melted into her mother's embrace.

"I'm sorry," Ming whispered, her voice barely audible.

"Shhh . . . you don't have to apologize. I'm your mother." Grandma took a step back and addressed Mei. "May Sun Yee guide you and keep you safe." She nodded, all business. Then she gestured toward the mirror. "One at a time, ladies. And quickly."

Mei's aunties formed a line behind Grandma.

"That's it? Mei-Mei's keeping the panda?" asked Auntie Chen.

"It's her life," Helen said. "Now move."

One by one, each woman stepped through the mirror, separating themselves from their panda spirits. The spirits faded into the forest.

Grandma was the last to leave. She looked around, taking it all in—the forest, the sky, and everything that the place meant to her and her family. She took a deep breath and stepped through the mirror with a dramatic flourish. Her red panda soared over their heads and disappeared into the dense forest.

Now it was just Mei and her mother. They both stepped up to the mirror. Mei squeezed her mother's hand.

"Go ahead," Mei said. "It's okay."

Without a word, Ming stepped into the mirror.

Mei braced herself as Ming's huge red panda spirit blew

past Mei. At the edge of the forest, Ming's panda spirit turned to look back at Mei. Mei gave a little wave and smiled. Then the spirit disappeared into the forest.

On the other side of the mirror, Ming paused, remembering her own struggles with her panda. She thought of Mei. "No, Mei-Mei, please!" She held out her hand. "Just come with me!"

Mei shook her head. "I'm changing, Mom. I'm finally figuring out who I am . . . but . . ." Tears formed at the corners of her eyes. "I'm scared it'll take me away from you."

"Me too," said Ming. "I see you, Mei-Mei. You try to make everyone happy but are so hard on yourself. And if I taught you that, I'm sorry. So don't hold back. For anyone."

Ming put her hand up to the mirror. Mei placed her hand against her mom's.

"The further you go, the prouder I'll be," said Ming with a smile.

As their hands touched, the mirror became opaque, and the red moon faded completely. Ming was gone. The mirror that had reflected Mei alone also disappeared.

Mei stood by herself under the full moon in the clearing. She sensed something behind her and turned. It was Sun Yee.

"I'm not going to regret this, am I?" Mei asked.

In a swirl of mist, Sun Yee became a glorious, celestial panda flying in the air. She catapulted toward Mei.

Mei transformed into a panda, and Sun Yee flew her above the bamboo forest. They floated before the full moon. Sun Yee touched her head to Mei's, and everything faded to white.

Chapter 19

A month had passed since Pandapocalypse 2002 (aka Mei's and Ming's growing pains). The city skyline sparkled, reflecting the rays of the sun. The stadium could be seen in the distance under heavy construction. Mei and Ming prayed in the temple in front of Sun Yee's altar.

Suddenly, something went *Beep! Beep!*

It was Mei's Robaire Junior. The digital pet was hanging from Ming's neck, where her pendant used to be. At the stadium, Mr. Gao had to put Ming's panda spirit into something.

"This thing's hungry all the time," Ming said as she pressed a button to feed Robaire Junior. "Eat up, little one!"

Mei laughed, happy that Mom had gotten Robaire Junior. It could have been Grandma, who instead was cursed with a 4*Town necklace that had a glittery and unlucky number four as a pendant!

Ming and Mei got up from the floor. "You ready?" Mei said.

Ming grinned. "Let's do this!"

Mei *poof*ed into her panda self and flung open the temple gates to a crowd anxious to get in, many wearing Red Panda Girl shirts and hats. They were true fans.

"Hello," Ming said. "Welcome to our temple."

"What up, Toronto! Get in here!" said Mei.

Things at the temple had never been better as visitors of all ages and backgrounds poured in. The courtyard bustled with activity. Jin led a tour. "Our temple is the oldest in Toronto," he said as he passed through with a group, "and the only one that's home to the Great Red Panda."

After each tour finished, visitors stuffed cash into a donation box with a sign that read ALL PROCEEDS GO TO THE REBUILDING OF THE STADIUM! The panda-hustle Pandameter had been repurposed with a meter that went into the tens of thousands of dollars.

Panda Mei took photos with families, fans, and tourists. "Say 'bamboo leaves'!"

"Bamboo leaves!" everyone repeated.

At that moment, Miriam, Priya, Abby, and Tyler walked through the gates.

"Guys!" Mei exclaimed.

"Yo," Priya said.

"Hey, furball," Tyler said.

They all bumped hips, then wiggled their fingers together.

"Ready to get your karaoke on?" Miriam asked.

Mei *poof*ed back into a girl, except for her ears and tail.

"You know it!" Then she turned to her parents. "Bye, Mom! Bye, Dad!"

Ming hurried over to her daughter. "Hold on! You're not going out like that, are you?"

"My panda, my choice, Mom." She rolled her eyes and then hugged Ming. "I'll be back before dinner, okay?"

Ming relented. "Fine." She addressed Mei's friends. "You're welcome to join us."

Mei's besties nodded enthusiastically. "For Mr. Lee's cooking? Uh—yeah!" said Miriam.

As the friends walked through the courtyard toward the gates, Ming called out to them, "Don't load up on junk!"

Mei turned to wave at her father. "Thanks for covering for me, Dad!"

"Have fun!" said Jin as he put on Mei's old panda costume.

The friends gabbed about which songs they would sing at karaoke. When they reached the gates, Mei looked back at her parents one last time. Ming and Jin were chatting with visitors. She made eye contact with her mom, and they smiled at each other.

Sometimes Mei missed how things were, but now she knew that nothing in her life could stay the same forever. Mei went through the gates with her friends as Ming brought a tour group to see a photo hanging in a place of honor: the ultimate selfie of Ming, Jin, Miriam, Priya, Abby, Tyler, the aunties, Grandma, Mr. Gao, and 4*Town crowded around a blissed-out Panda Mei, who was cheek-to-cheek with Robaire.

The photo was one of the best things Mei had in her whole life because it captured her amazing family and friends, who loved her no matter how beastly she could be.

And Mei knew, better than anyone else, that everyone had an inner beast. Everyone had a messy, loud, and weird part of themselves hidden away. And sometimes, to figure out who you are, you just have to let it out!